Every Single Vow

S.J. Chaynie

Cover design by S.J. Chaynie.

For the girls who just want a sweet talking cowboy who writes his own vows to put a ring on it.

This one's for you.

Contents

Blurb

I was ten years old when I met Cooper Mayson. Thirteen when he threw his first punch for me. Eighteen when my world crumbled beneath my feet and he promised he'd always take care of me. He was my constant. But with a last name like Sterling, and the tarnished reputation that came along with it, I've always kept him at arm's length. He was the golden boy with a loving family, and a ranch with a polished legacy. I was the girl with an absent mother, a father in prison, and a destination for nowhere. But now I was staring at a stranger. One that looked just like me. A little sister I knew nothing about. A child who had nowhere to go. I couldn't let her be another face lost in the system, but no judge in this town would give a child to me with my last name. It was hopeless. Until my best friend made me an offer. *To give me his*. Sounds simple enough. A temporary marriage so I can gain full custody, then have an amicable divorce. Problem is, I've been in love with my best friend since I was ten years old, and after only two weeks of being a Mayson, I realize, this fake marriage might not be as fake as I thought. Behind closed doors, the act doesn't end. Every kiss pulls me deeper. Every whisper heals my heart. It almost makes me believe I'm good enough for him. But if there's one soul in this world that I refuse to taint, it's *Cooper Mayson's.*

Note from author

This book may contain topics that are sensitive to some readers. Such as situations of child neglect and the death of a parent.

Prologue

Dakota

Ten years old

"Go go go," I whisper the words under my breath as I peer through the chain link fence.

The thunderous pounding of horses' feet sound all around me as the beautiful animals round the last curve, heading for the finish line.

I'm not supposed to be out by the track, but that stairwell Billy tells me to stay in is hot and smelly. I want to see the horses race. I love the way the crowd cheers and the way my heart beats faster when the horse I like wins. Race days are the rare days that Billy lets me go anywhere besides school. So even though I'll get in trouble later if he finds out that I snuck out of my hiding spot, it's worth it. He says kids aren't supposed to be here and I could get taken away. Some days I wish someone would take me. I might not be this sad all the time.

When the race is finished, I squeeze through the crowd, my toes cramping as I rush back to the door around the side of the building. I hate these sneakers. They're too small for my feet, but since Billy never has any money, he says we can't afford new ones. But he has money to come here and bet on those horses, and he has money to buy those brown bottles of beer that take up the whole fridge.

I've almost reached the door when I hear his voice.

"I thought I told you to stay put until I came back." His meaty palm catches my arm before he yanks me to face him.

"I was hot," I admit.

"You know the rules, Dakota," he scoffs. "I'm here to make money, not babysit." He glances around. "Did you at least make yourself useful if you weren't going to listen?"

I grit my teeth, biting the inside of my cheek in frustration as his eyes move over the sea of people.

"Empty your pockets." He narrows his eyes back on me.

Anger burns in my chest as I reach inside of my jean shorts, pulling out a wad of cash I had stolen from a few wallets. Most people are focused on the race, not the little girl next to them. Most of these men are in nice suit jackets, and don't pay attention to what hands are slipping into their pockets. A trick Billy taught me.

"Daddy's girl, huh?" He grins, snatching the bills from my hand.

Billy may be my dad, but he doesn't act like one. Not like the other dads at school. My small fingers clench when he takes the money. The money I was going to use to buy my lunch this week. We never have any food, not since mom left. All we have are those nasty brown bottles. I tried one once when I hadn't had anything to eat in two days and it made me puke.

He glances around again, shoving the money inside of his shirt pocket. "Let's go."

I can tell by the way he drags me along that he's irritated. Which means he lost. Again. And I'll be the one that pays for it.

On the way home, my body bounces with every bump we hit in his old Chevy truck. There's no air conditioner, and the Texas sun is shining directly though my window, making sweat bead at my temples. Before we make it home, Billy pulls the truck over in front of a gas station. He doesn't speak as he opens his door. I unbuckle quickly, using all of my strength to nudge open the heavy door so I can jump out. The jingle of the bell sounds just as I catch up to him at the door, and he scowls over his shoulder at me. I follow closely, hoping he'll let me get something to eat. My stomach was growling the whole way into town. He opens a cooler, grabbing a pack of those brown bottles again, before he moves up to the counter and gruffly asks for a pack of cigarettes. I hate his voice. It sounds scratchy.

My gaze drifts to the man that walks in the door, a boy that looks around my age trotting behind him. He's wearing a cowboy hat and nice boots. I'd give anything to have boots like that.

"I'm hungry." I tug on Billy's shirt tail. "Can I get something to eat? Some chips?"

He ignores me, unfolding the same wad of cash he took from me earlier.

"No," he says before he flicks through the bills.

My stomachs growls. "Please?"

I usually don't ask for anything because he gets mad, but my stomach is starting to hurt.

"I said no, girl. Open your damn ears."

I sink back, my arms crossing as I watch him pay for his things, then he stalks away from me.

With a heavy feeling in my chest, I watch him go, before glancing at the man behind the counter.

"Have a good day." He smiles weakly.

"You too," I mutter.

I move slowly, pushing open the glass door. Before I'm off of the sidewalk, the bell jingles behind me. I peek over my shoulder to see the boy in the cowboy hat.

"Hey, what's your name?" He asks.

I blink, looking at the prettiest blue eyes that I've ever seen.

"Dakota." I stand taller, turning to face him.

He holds out a bag of BBQ chips. "Here you go."

I frown, but he just grabs my hand and places the bag in my palm. "You're hungry."

I stare down at the bag of chips and for the first time I feel tears well, and it's not because I'm scared. It's because I'm thankful.

I meet his eyes again and he smiles.

"Thank you." I clutch the bag to my chest. "What's your name?" I ask.

He tips his hat with a goofy smile. "I'm Cooper. Cooper Mayson."

Chapter One

Cooper

Present day

"So, you're officially going to be my brother-in-law?" I ask Maddox, who knocks back the rest of his drink as we sit at the bar of the Mayson Jar.

The restaurant my aunt owns doubles as a dance hall most evenings and since the guy next to me just slipped a diamond ring on my sister's finger, we came here to celebrate.

"As quick as she will let me." He chuckles.

I slap a palm against his back. "Congrats, man."

Maddox Sheppard had been a part of my family for years, regardless of if he's blood or not, and I couldn't have picked a better guy for Ivy. He's the head operator for the bucking bulls owned by our family ranch, and we've been buddies for years.

"You buying my drinks tonight, cowboy?" A teasing voice comes from my right.

Dakota Sterling leans an elbow on the bar, her long dark hair cascading over her bare collarbone. Her blue eyes twinkle, the colorful tattoo across her shoulder drawing my attention. She shrugs it up a fraction and smiles. It slams into me with the speed of a freight train. It always does. It has since the first time I saw her. *At ten years old.*

My best friend laughs, and I reach up to pinch her chin between my fingers. "Don't I always get your drinks?"

She smirks, then leans in so she can see past me, and calls out to Maddox who just started talking to Parker, my cousin.

"Epic show, Shep." She gives a thumbs up. "Our girl is all smiles."

My sister is currently laughing as Clyde, the oldest ranch hand that we have twirls her around the dance floor.

"That's my goal. Keep her smiling." Maddox lifts his drink.

Dakota smiles and leans back on her elbows next to me. "She deserves it."

I motion to Shorty, the bartender who nods when I point to Dakota. He knows what she drinks, just like I do. I watch her profile as she scans the room, and I'm silently praying that some fucker doesn't come ask her to dance. If I have to sit back and watch one more man spin her around that floor, or take her home, I'll end up with a prison sentence. Which is the last thing Dakota needs considering that's where her father is.

I've kept my feelings to myself. Played the best friend role for as long as I can remember. But my *feelings* for the dark haired beauty next to me are anything but platonic. Dakota is a wild card. A woman that wears her armor proud and true. She's tough. She's loud. She's impulsive. But that's only to hide that little girl inside that's so used to being broken. I would know. I met that little girl first, and somewhere along the way, she got sick of being her. Sick of letting that worthless man rule her happiness. Her joy. It wasn't overnight, but my best friend bloomed into this confident, ruthless, loyal, woman who would burn down the entire world for the people she loved. It was potent. Evident in everything she did, but there was still that small part of her that she could never fully extract. The part that reminded her of her past. Of where she came from. And that part is the only thing that has kept me strictly in the friend zone.

"Tequila Sunset." Shorty drops her drink down on the bar top.

She spins to grab it, her lips wrapping around the straw. "Thanks, Coop." She winks. "I owe you."

I take the fresh drink from her hand, smiling as she scoffs in annoyance.

"You do." I sit her drink down on the bar. "You owe me a dance, Birdie."

Chapter Two

Dakota

The sign to the Mayson Ranch comes into view as the low rumble of the cattle guard sounds below us. I'm riding shotgun, while Ivy sits in the backseat with her *fiancé,* Maddox. They got engaged less than four hours ago, in the middle of the arena at the annual Mayson Ridge Rodeo. If anyone deserves the fairytale ending its Ivy Mayson. Her cowboy dropped to a knee, dirt and all, and asked her in front of the entire town, along with the rest of the world to be his wife. It was everything a girl dreams of.

My eyes move over to the driver. My other best friend, Cooper. He has a wrist draped over the steering wheel, his other arm resting on the console. Another person that deserves the happy ending. *He deserves the world.* But people like me, we don't get those. We don't get the luxury of fate. The white picket fence, two and a half kids, and two matching rocking chairs on a back porch. As much as it stings, I've come to terms with it.

The long gravel drive feels more like home than the ratty old trailer I lived in for the majority of my life. I can't count the times I crept down this driveway. Whether it was in the middle of the afternoon, or the dead of the night. I could never describe the exact emotion it brought on. *Peace? Relief?*

We pull up to the farmhouse that's being completely rebuilt. A few months ago, a fire took out Cooper's childhood home, along with some of the pastureland. It was a financial hit to the ranch, but after it was concluded that foul play was involved by the biggest crook in town, the Mayson's were able to claim the insurance money and are in the process of rehabilitating this ranch to a better version of itself.

Cooper slams the truck into park and reaches over to silently unclip my seat belt. I roll my eyes before I begin to sing out loud the lyrics to my favorite song with the futile attempt to drown out the feeling that Cooper Mayson stirs within my hollow chest. I've been working on ignoring it for years. I've yet to accomplish it.

I pull the latch, jumping down from the truck as we all make our exit. My steps are slightly off balance, the tequila still doing its job.

"Whoa!" Cooper's tone of voice causes me to end my lyrical ensemble mid chorus. "Who the hell are you?" He growls.

My boots are ambling forward as quick as I can, rounding the hood to see a small figure stalk down the front steps of the unfinished farmhouse.

"I'm looking for Dakota Sterling." The lanky preteen blows a pink bubble, before she tucks the gum back into her mouth.

Something about her is oddly familiar.

"I'm Dakota Sterling." I move a fraction, my shoulders tight as I take her in.

Long dark hair.

Big blue eyes.

Just like mine.

"Sweet. I'm Arizona Sterling. Mind if I crash?" She asks casually.

Sterling.

I frown. "Who are you?"

She hikes her black backpack up onto her shoulder. "I figured she didn't tell you." She rolls her eyes with a sigh. "Surprise. I'm your little sister."

I blink, before I dart my eyes to Cooper.

"Excuse me?" I ask.

Damn, this is some strong tequila. I'm pretty sure this kid just said she was my sister.

"I'm your sister," she repeats. "Bea Sterling is my mother." She waves a hand. "Well, was."

Bea. The woman who gave birth to me. Half ass raised me. Then left me.

"What do you mean was?"

"She's dead," she replies with a blank expression.

"What?" I croak.

"Yeah. Died three days ago. Overdose." She glances at her chipped nails. "She hooked up with some biker guy in New Orleans. I think she started back on the hard stuff."

I blink again, looking around to make sure I'm not hallucinating.

"How old are you?" Cooper is the one to ask as he moves to stand next to me.

"I'm twelve."

Twelve.

My neck feels hot.

"Why..." I take a breath. "Why are you here?"

"She told me if something ever happened to her to go find you. Said I could find you in Mayson Ridge, which by the way is like the most boring place I've ever been and I've only been here for like six hours."

Cooper's palm lands on the small of my back, and I can feel him rubbing light circles. He's always the calm in the storm. And for some reason, I'm always the hurricane.

"Anyway, I asked around for you, and I was told I could find you here." She shrugs.

"How did you get here?" I ask. "Where's your dad?"

How the hell did a twelve year old girl travel alone from New Orleans?

"Took the bus. And as for the dad, never met him." She crosses her arms.

"Umm," I start, then look over to Ivy. "So, you have no other family?" I press.

"Nope." She pops the p, pursing her lips.

"Arizona, you said?" Ivy smiles, doing her thing while I stand frozen in the dirt like an idiot.

"Yeah, but you can call me Ari," she answers.

"I'm Ivy." She motions her hand. "This is Maddox, my fiancé. And this is Cooper, my brother."

“Cool.” She hikes her bag up again. “Not to sound like a brat, but can you point me to where I can sleep? I don’t even mind the floor. Just somewhere dry with AC.”

A swift pang hits my chest. The look in her eyes, the coolness in her tone. She’s got the act down. The mask in place. I would know. I’ve been wearing it for years. But the broken can always recognize the broken and my heart nearly cracks down the middle when I realize what I’m looking at.

A mirror.

Chapter Three

Cooper

I can tell by the look of pure shock on Dakota's face that she had no idea Arizona existed. She hadn't even heard from, nor seen Bea since she left one night when Dakota was eight. Just *poof*. Gone.

"Sure." I clear my throat, tilting my head to Ivy to let her know I'll need her help. "Let's get you inside and we can sort all of this out in the morning." I smile, hoping she isn't weirded out by a strange man offering her a place to sleep.

"Thanks." It's barely there, but I can see the slight relief in her frail shoulders.

She looks so much like Dakota did at that age it's uncanny. Everything except their frame. Where Dakota is tall, all long legs, this girl is on the shorter side. But the eyes and hair are a spitting image.

Reminds me of why I call Dakota *Birdie.* That's what she reminded me of that day at the gas station. Big blue eyes. Skinny and frail. Jet black hair.

"Of course," Dakota shrills before turning to face me with wide eyes.

"You can stay in the guest room," I offer before pointing toward the new cabin I had built after the fire.

Arizona nods, and Ivy steps in to lead her the rest of the way, knowing Dakota needs a minute.

"I'll take you." Ivy smiles. "I like your shoes."

Arizona mutters something under her breath, but I don't hear it because I've already turned my attention to the woman beside me.

"She doesn't have to stay with you, Coop." Dakota runs a hand through her hair, seconds away from a manic episode.

"She can. And you are too," I add.

"Me?"

"She's a kid. Not only is she a young girl, but she'll be in a house alone with a strange man and I'd rather not make her uncomfortable."

I reach out and press my thumb over the wrinkle of her brows. "And quite frankly I'm not sure I trust her. We don't know her from Adam, and I don't particularly like the idea of her being alone with you. I would rather confirm her story first."

"Right." She closes her eyes.

"Hey," I whisper. Her eyes fly open. "What's going on in there?" I lift my hand, my finger tapping her temple.

"My mom…" she pauses before shaking her head. "Can we just get her settled and talk in the morning?"

She may seem like a woman without a care in the world, but she holds more care in that wild heart than any other person I've met. It's just guarded so well, that if you blink you'll miss it.

"Take my bed." I turn to walk across the gravel drive and to my cabin that sits just a beat away from the horse stables.

"Coop," she starts.

"Kota." I cut her off. "My bed. I'll be on the couch."

I would never put her on the couch and I'm not above admitting that I'm a sappy motherfucker and the thought of her perfume clinging to my sheets just does something to me.

"Whatever you say, boss," she mumbles before I hear her boots following behind me.

When we enter my cabin, I can hear Ivy chatting away with Arizona in my guest room.

"Bathroom is down the hall," she tells her. "There's a big tile shower if you need to use it."

"Dope," Arizona responds.

Dakota chuckles behind me as we walk through the living room.

"Dope?" I mutter.

"She's practically a teenager." Dakota scoots past me in the hallway, entering the guest room. "They have their own language."

"Do you need anything?" Dakota asks Arizona.

"This is good." The girl twirls in a small circle. "I don't need much."

I can see the deep set of Dakota's brows again. She's thinking. Flustered. And probably pissed at her mom along with the shock of her death.

"I'll be just down the hall." Dakota runs her hands over the pockets of her jeans. "You can shower if you need to."

"Towels are in the cabinet," I chime in. "Soap and some hair stuff is under the sink."

Arizona nods as I press a hand to Dakota's lower back and tilt my chin to Ivy.

"Well, goodnight Ari. It's nice to meet you," Ivy says before we leave the room and pause in the living room.

"So what exactly is going on?" Maddox stands in the doorway of the kitchen, a slice of leftover pizza in hand.

Dakota plops down on my couch, leaning her head back with her eyes closed. "Just a good ole Sterling family reunion."

Chapter Four

Dakota

The sun shines through the navy curtain shielding the window as I lay staring at the ceiling. I couldn't sleep. I couldn't believe the fact I had a *sister.* A sibling I'd always begged for, but mom had made it clear that she didn't even want me, much less anyone else to take care of. *Yeah, Bea Sterling was a regular June Cleaver.* I was trying to dig deep. Trying to psychoanalyze why I haven't shed a tear over her passing. It could be because she left me with that monster. Left me knowing his temper. Knowing how neglectful he was. But she didn't even care, and as horrible as it sounds, a part of me doesn't care that she's not around anymore either.

I turn my head, my nose connecting with the soft cotton pillowcase where Cooper lays his head every night. It smells like a cowboy, leather, and spice. It smells like a man who probably did unthinkable things in these very sheets. That thought has my stomach rolling, so I push the covers off of me before climbing out of the bed. That's one visual I can't handle today. *The thought of Cooper with another woman.* Just because I know that I can't have him, doesn't mean that it doesn't sting when someone else does. *It really fucking stings, actually.*

I take a few minutes to brush my teeth with my toothbrush he has set aside for me when I occasionally sleep over. He probably has a whole slew for his other overnight guests, but I push that intrusive thought away too. A quick splash of water on my face and my hair pulled back into a ponytail has me ready to face whatever shit show is waiting outside this bedroom door.

Stepping into the hallway, I already smell the scent of bacon as I tiptoe down the brand new hardwood floors. If there's one thing about Cooper that is distinctly different from me, it's that he's a morning person. Infuriatingly chipper before the sun is up and insists on cooking a full fledged breakfast along with making the world's worst coffee imaginable.

"Morning," he calls when I walk into the room.

"Morning," I mumble back, reaching into the fridge for the orange juice.

My eyes take in the kitchen, before I peer around the living room.

No sign of Arizona.

"Any movement this morning?" I ask, flaring my eyes with a tilt of my head in the direction of the guest bedroom.

"She's not a wild hog, Kota. She's a child." He flings a hand towel over his shoulder as he carries a full plate of crispy bacon over to the island.

I glare at him, before I sit down on a bar stool. "I'm aware."

He then moves to the microwave, retracting a pile of Texas shaped waffles.

"Your strawberries are already cut up in that bowl." He motions.

"You're going to make a fine housewife one day, Coop." I drag the bowl to me while he shoots me a wink.

A wink I've tried years to endure without my stomach fluttering, but here I sit, about to flutter off of this stool.

"You didn't sleep, did you?" He makes his own plate before planting himself next to me.

He was already fully dressed. Starched jeans, a paisley pearl snap with the top two buttons undone. *Always* the top two, showing off the sterling silver chain that he always wore. His scuffed up boots were on his feet, but he hadn't put on his hat. His hair was still slightly damp; the dirty blonde strands tossed around carelessly on his head as he shovels a bite of waffles into his mouth.

"Is that code for you look like shit?" I pop a strawberry into my mouth then nudge my shoulder with his. "Thank you for breakfast by the way."

He smiles, my favorite dimple forming on his right cheek. "Always take care of you, Kota. You know this."

And he did. Always.

"And you could never look like shit. I've seen you at your worst. Remember the county fair circa 2018?"

"God, don't remind me." I groan.

That night involved way too much vodka and corn dogs. *Gross.*

I sigh as I reach for a piece of bacon. "What do I do?"

"About what?" He stabs a few pieces of his waffle.

"About global warming." I roll my eyes. "About the preteen currently sleeping in your guest room, Cooper."

"First you need to confirm what she said about your mom. You can call the coroner's office in New Orleans, or I'm sure find records online."

That would be the easy part. But what about after? Where does she go? Who takes care of her? There's not a chance in hell I'm equipped for this kind of responsibility, right? I can't even keep up with a set of keys much less a human.

"Ok." I pinch the bridge of my nose, trying to ward off a slight headache. The tequila from last night was wreaking havoc on my body today. "Thanks for letting us stay. I'll take her to the trailer today."

My current living situation may seem flighty to some, but residing in the living quarters of my horse trailer gave me the freedom to travel and to save money. Cooper never liked it, which is how I ended up parking it at the Mayson Ranch as its home base.

"I don't like it," he says.

"She's my sister. Not your problem."

"Well considering *you've* been my problem since we were ten years old, that makes *her* my problem via blood relation."

I lift a brow. "I'm your problem?"

"Every fucking day," he mumbles.

I flip him off, but he just snatches my hand, tugging me in for a hug that I pretend I can't stand.

"I hate you sometimes," I hiss as I push at his chest.

He chuckles. "Lies. You love me."

More than anything.

"Dream on," I scoff.

A throat clears and I jerk at the sound behind me. Arizona stands in her clothes from last night, her eyebrows lifted with amusement.

"Morning." Cooper pushes to his feet. "Hungry?"

"Sure." She shrugs a shoulder casually, but I can hear her stomach growl from here.

"Get whatever you want. Plates are there." Cooper waves a hand. "Forks are in the drawer by the fridge."

Her eyes cut to mine but then move to the spread on the island. I'm watching her approach with the timidness of a deer when a light touch lands on my shoulder.

Cooper nods in the direction of the porch, so I follow after telling Arizona I'll just be a second.

When I close the door behind me, he drops his cowboy hat on his head.

"Let me run out to the barn. Make sure everything is sorted. You know Sundays are chill. When I get done, we can make those calls."

I nod, the heavy weight settling in.

My mom is dead.

I have a sister.

"You don't have to rearrange your day for me. I can handle it," I tell him.

He ignores my comment per usual, then leans in and presses his lips to my temple. Like he does every time he leaves me. "Keeping my word, Kota."

I watch his form travel down the stairs, across the gravel, and into the horse barn.

Keeping his word.

He always has.

Since the day I met him.

I'd give anything to be the woman who lived life right beside him. *With him.* But some things just aren't in the cards for some of us. Some of us have bad blood running through our veins. Darkness in our roots. A darkness I could never allow to snuff out his light.

Chapter Five

Cooper

My foot is barely over the threshold to the barn when I hear hooves pounding the ground behind me. I glance over my shoulder to see Dale, my deaf blue heeler none the wiser to my brother Ryder, and his horse Mags, angrily crossing the pasture. Everything Ryder does looks angry, riding a horse isn't any different. Neither is him already being on horseback at the crack of dawn and clearly not sleeping.

"Cooper." He comes to an abrupt stop right before he plows over Dale who ambles out of the way at the last second.

"Good morning, brother." I toss my arms on the top rail of the fence. "You're up early."

He runs a hand over his chin. "We need to start moving the herd."

"I agree. It won't be today though," I answer.

"That's fine. Needs to start this week or next though. It will take us a few days just to get everything accounted for." He shifts while Mags blows a puff of air through her nose.

"Hey girl." I run my hand up her nose. "I have some things to handle today. I won't be around much. You need anything holler at Clyde."

"Where you going?" He asks.

I blow out a breath. "Dakota." I pause. "Her little sister showed up at the ranch last night."

He lifts a brow. "Little sister?"

"Yeah. Apparently, Bea managed to procreate again after leaving Dakota in the dust."

"Why she here?"

"Bea overdosed. Dead. The girl is twelve, traveled all the way from New Orleans. Has no other family." I take off my hat and run a hand through my hair. "Need to help Kota get all that figured out."

He's quiet for a moment before he surprises me. "Need anything let me know."

Then he snickers at Mags and trots off.

I peer out over the farmland. Most of it finally grew back from the fire. The fire that almost destroyed everything my family had built. The Mayson Ranch has been in my family for generations. It's been burned into my brain and blood since I took my first breath. I was a rancher. Through and through, and I wanted nothing more than to make this place better. A legacy that will be remembered long after I'm gone.

Turning back toward the barn, I pick up my pace and step inside to check the horses. Buster, my bay horse sits in his stall, appearing to be half asleep like he always is. Sugarfoot, Ivy's horse automatically neighs in greeting, creating a musical ensemble from the remaining stalls that house the rest of the ranch horses.

"Morning to y'all too." I chuckle.

"If it isn't the horse whisperer." Clyde stands by the tack room, a cup of coffee in hand.

We both know who the real horse whisperer is. It's the dark haired woman who slept in my bed last night. I push the thought away, not needing to get a hard on in front of a man who I practically consider my grandpa.

"Clyde. Surprised you're still kicking," I tease.

For his early seventies, the man still handles a horse like a champ.

"Can still run circles around you, boy," he tosses back but there's no heat.

This happened to be our love language.

Insults and sarcasm.

"I've got some things going on today. Figured I'd let the horses graze in the north pasture for a bit. Stretch their legs."

"No problem. Do what you got to do." He sips his coffee.

"Thanks, Clyde. I'll have my phone on me."

He salutes me before I leave the barn, making my way back to my cabin. A few guys are already at work on the farmhouse.

"Hey, Tom." I lift a hand to the contractor that's measuring a cabinet.

"Morning, Cooper." He tucks the tape measure back into his tool belt. "Making progress."

"Looking good. Got an end date?" I ask, resting my hands in my pockets as I approach.

"Hopefully one more month. I have instructions by Emmett to make sure your mama can cook Thanksgiving dinner in her new kitchen."

I chuckle. "That would make her entire year."

Ruthie Mayson was big on family. Thanksgiving was one of her favorite holidays and don't even get me started on Christmas.

"Come by later today. I should have the kitchen cabinets installed."

"Perfect." I reach a hand out. "We appreciate you, man."

Turning on my heel, I head for the house, Dale hobbling by my side.

I have a feeling things are about to get crazy. And I'm here for it.

Chapter Six

Dakota

I watch as Arizona practically inhales three waffles.

"Want some juice?" I offer.

"Yes. Thank you." She clears her throat, before placing her fork on her empty plate.

I pour her a glass and try to figure out how to start this awkward conversation.

"So, um...you and Bea...I mean mom," I correct. This is harder than I expected. "Where have y'all been living? New Orleans?"

She drinks half of the juice before shrugging. "We'd been in New Orleans for about five years. Before that we were in Houston."

"Where did you live?" I ask before taking her empty plate to the sink.

"When she died, we'd been staying with her friend. I didn't care for Craig. He looked at me funny."

My chest squeezes, pain lacing my bones. I knew what that meant. She didn't even have to say it.

"That's why you came here? You didn't want to stay with her friend?"

"No. He was gross." She finishes off the juice. "Mom had plenty of friends. That's who we usually stayed with. She wasn't one who liked to hold a job or do anything remotely responsible."

I blink, shocked at how mature she is for twelve years old. But I understand it. When you raise yourself, you don't have a choice. Maturity is unavoidable. I know exactly what that's like. To have your childhood robbed because your caretaker can't act like a real parent.

"Have you..." I shift on my feet. "Have you always been with her?"

I'm shocked the school she attended never questioned anything.

"I had to go stay with a foster family once for a few weeks." She glances at me. "Let's just say staying with Creepy Craig would have been the better option."

I study her face. She puts on a front, but I can see the fear in her eyes. The uncertainty. The scared little girl inside. *I see me.*

The silence hangs, and my chest tightens.

"Dakota," she says quietly.

It's the first time she's actually addressed me.

"Yeah?"

"I know it's a lot to ask but, could you.... could you not send me back?" She holds my stare.

Blue eyes.

Dark hair.

A neglected soul.

And the answer is crystal clear. I might not know how it's going to work, and I might end up being a really crappy sister, but there's no way I'm sending this child anywhere.

She came to me. And I'm going to do what my mother should have done in the first place.

Love her.

The door to the cabin opens, and Cooper steps in. I have to swallow past the lump in my throat at the feeling of security that washes over me.

"Hey girls. Get you plenty to eat Arizona?" He asks.

"Yep," she answers.

"The waffles? Best you ever had right?" He grins.

She scoffs. "Please. You obviously haven't been to the Lilly Pad Motel continental breakfast."

I let a laugh bubble up. This girl has wit. I like it.

"You wound me, Ari." He holds a hand to his chest.

"Truth hurts." She swings her legs from the barstool. "Mind if I shower? I was too exhausted last night."

"Not at all." Cooper slips off his hat, hanging it on the dining chair. "Take your time."

Arizona leaves the kitchen, and sudden tears spring to my eyes.

"Hey, Hey. What's this?" Cooper moves to me immediately, his arms already reaching for me.

I step into them, the warmth causing the tears to spill over. "She...what she's been through."

"What did she tell you?" He runs a hand up my back.

"Enough." I sniff. "If she really has no one...." I lean back, and peer up at him. "I know I'm not mother material. I know I'm impulsive and can't keep up with my own ass if it wasn't attached." I close my eyes. "But she needs someone, Cooper."

I feel his thumb swipe at one of my tears.

"She needs me," I croak.

"Okay then." His palm slides down my arm. "Let's see what we need to do."

We.

I nod, my hands coming up to wipe my face. "You tell anyone I cried, and I'll shrink all of your favorite pearl snaps," I threaten.

He laughs, before he pulls out his phone. "Your tears are safe with me, Birdie."

The comment makes my heart flutter, because he's always been the only one that I allowed to see them.

"You want to make the call or me?" He asks.

I blow out a long breath.

"I need to." I take his phone and hover my finger over the New Orleans Coroner's Office knowing that one confirmation, could change everything.

Chapter Seven

Dakota

"She's asleep," I whisper as I come down the hallway.

Poor thing obviously hasn't been sleeping since she crashed not long after her shower.

Cooper is at the kitchen table, his fingers sliding across the keyboard.

My nerves where finally starting to settle. After the phone call that confirmed my mother was in fact, deceased, Cooper and I spent two hours looking up Texas law for gaining custody of a minor.

"She's probably exhausted from the travel alone." Cooper closes his laptop. "I emailed Norman. He's agreed to meet with us tomorrow for legal advice."

Norman was the lawyer for the ranch, but he dabbled in all sorts of law.

"Thanks, Coop." I squeeze his forearm that's propped up on the table. "I owe you big."

"I'll be creative in your repayment." His cheeky grin has me slapping his arm. "I'm not one of your buckle bunnies, Mayson."

His eyebrows raise. "When's the last time you saw me with a buckle bunny?"

"Oh, I don't know." I wave my hand. "Last night."

He narrows his eyes. "Name one."

"Alison."

I try not to let my jealously flare, because it's absurd. But watching her flirt with him has always unnerved me. She's blonde. Pretty. And perfect for him. No scandalous family. No *baggage.*

Ugh.

"She spoke to me for all of five seconds," he scoffs. "Besides, how would you have known? You were pretty occupied with that scum bag, Vickerson."

I lean my head back on a laugh. "Seriously? We work together. I train his horses."

"He wanted you to train more than that," he mutters.

"You don't like him?" I press, trying not to laugh.

"Fuck no." He pushes up from the table. "He's an arrogant prick."

I watch as he paces the kitchen, before he snatches up a toothpick from the container on the counter and drops it in his mouth.

"Ok." I lift my hands. "No need to get twitchy."

Before he can fire back a remark, Ivy is bursting through the front door with Laiken trailing behind her.

"We came for an update." Ivy smiles, a casserole in hand. "And we have supper."

Cooper takes it from her hands, helping himself as Ivy and Laiken climb onto the sofa with me. These two are the definition of *ride or die.* I met Ivy through Cooper, and Laiken through Ivy. We've been thick as thieves ever since, and I wouldn't have it any other way. Ivy grips my hand, her bright smile always a comfort. Laiken's kind spirit is one of those that makes you feel like you are wrapped up in your favorite blanket by a fire on a cold winter day. My friends are everything I'm not. Ivy can talk to anyone. Smart as a whip and loyal to a fault. Laiken has always been the center. The gravity. The sound mind. The nurturer. And I was well….*me.*

"How is she?" Ivy asks.

"Good. Fed, showered, and resting." I tuck my bare feet beneath me.

"Does she need anything?" Laiken asks.

"I will probably need to get her a few sets of clothes. Some toiletries." I glance back at Cooper. "I really won't know what's next until we see the attorney tomorrow and he tells us the process."

"If you need me to, I can take her to town to get those things while you and Coop meet with him."

"Thanks, Ives." I smile.

"Will she go to foster care?" Laiken's gaze drifts over to Ivy.

I shake my head. "No. I can't let her go back."

"Go back?" Ivy's eyes soften. "She's been before?"

"Yeah." I swallow. "Not a good experience." I finally have the courage to say it. "I want her to stay with me."

I'm not sure what I expected, but Ivy launching herself at me was not it.

"I'm so proud of you," she sobs.

Laiken joins next, her arms wrapping around us both. "Me too. We're right here. Whatever you need."

"Thank you." I let my gaze track over to Cooper and then I mouth the words to him across the room. *Thank you.* Who knew that meeting him at a gas station at ten years old would lead me here. To this family.

Chapter Eight

Dakota

"So Norman is going to tell us what we need to do?" I ask, wringing my hands as I step a boot onto the curb.

"Yes. I trust Norman. He knows the law forwards and backwards. He won't steer us wrong."

I nod, breathing out a sharp breath. Norman was never downright ugly to me, but he had friends. Judges and law men in this town that hated seeing the name *Sterling* on their radar.

"Relax." Cooper's hand brushes against my lower back. "It's just a conversation, Birdie."

He only calls me *Birdie* when he's soothing me. He knows I'm getting anxious. The nickname is always like a balm to my soul, and

I soak in the feel of his touch before he opens the door to the old building next to the hardware store.

"Good morning." Mrs. Lane smiles and motions to the left. "Mr. Grisham is still in a meeting, but you can go into the third office on the right." Her smile slightly waivers when she glances at me.

I smile back, trying not to take offense.

Cooper's steps lead me down the hall, and as we turn into the third office on the right, my steps falter.

"Coop!"

My eyes narrow, the force so strong I have to reign in the urge to roll them at the enthusiastic voice. Kyra Grisham, the woman who's done everything but strip naked in front of Cooper to snag his attention sits behind the desk.

"I hope you don't mind meeting with me. Dad's meeting ran long, and he gave me the cliff notes and told me to advise then bring him up to speed."

"Morning, Kyra. No problem." Cooper's boots scuff along the floor, while she practically eye fucks him the entire short trip to the leather back chair.

It takes everything I have not to comment.

He's not mine.

But he is. *Kind of.*

"You finally off on your own?" Cooper asks, dropping down in the chair.

"Passed the bar last month." She blushes. "Big girl now."

Oh, for fucks sake.

I sit in the chair next to Cooper, still completely invisible to the supposed *lawyer* that just giggled like we were in fourth grade.

"That's great." Cooper crosses a boot covered ankle over one knee. "Then you should be able to point Kota in the right direction."

At the mention of my name, Kyra finally acknowledges my presence.

"Dakota." She forms a tight smile. "Good to see you."

"Congratulations, Kyra. Your dad must be proud." I give a genuine smile, because despite what everyone thinks, I'm *not* my father.

"Thanks." She glances back at Cooper, who's gaze I can feel on the side of my face.

"So, I was informed you were needing some legal information on family law. Gaining custody of a child?" She asks.

"Yes. Just the general process and requirements," he answers.

"I had no idea you had a child." She swallows.

"Oh, I don't." Cooper barks out a laugh. "It's for Kota."

Her eyes widen. "You have a child?"

"No." I clench my fists. "I have a sister."

"Okay." She leans up, her hand reaching for a pen. "And where is the mother?"

"Dead," I say, keeping my eyes on hers. "I'm the child's only living family member. She's twelve years old."

Kyra blinks, her expression changing from surprise to pity. "I'm sorry to hear that. About your mother."

"She left when I was eight, and when she was still around, she was never home anyway. No skin off my back." My hands wring together, my pulse starting to thud.

My leg involuntarily bounces, the sign I'm about to spiral and my breathing increases.

The gentle touch of Cooper's hand makes my leg still, and he locks eyes with me.

"Dakota doesn't want her in the system. We know how that goes with overcrowding. I understand not everyone has ill intentions, but it's something we don't want to chance. Arizona should be with family."

Kyra rolls her lips. "I see. Well, the first thing we would need is to provide the death certificate for her mother, then you would need to file a SAPCR with the court. Once that is filed, you will need to provide proof of a stable home environment. Physical, emotional, and financial stability as well."

Kyra turns to me. "I know you train horses. But do you have a steady income? Are you still living in that trailer? With your last name..."

"Wait a minute." Cooper's sharp tone has Kyra jolting. "What the fuck does that have to do with anything?"

"Well, I just mean, for a single woman, with her family history. It's very unlikely a judge will..."

"A judge will what? Not grant custody because she had a shit father?"

"Cooper. It's fine," I hiss under my breath.

Honestly, I expected this. I knew it wouldn't be a walk in the park.

"No." His jaw hardens. "So, you're telling me that even if she was the absolute best person to care for Arizona, a judge would dismiss her because of her last name?"

"Cooper..." Kyra begins, but he shakes his head.

His body shifts, then a look passes over his face before he freezes. A slow grin spreads across his face before he tenderly reaches out and intertwines his fingers with mine.

"Well Kyra, fortunately for us, that won't be an issue in this situation."

I frown, not understanding his direction.

"I'm not following." Kyra sits up straighter.

"Her name won't be Sterling." Cooper smirks.

I jerk my gaze in his direction and I'm pretty sure my body levitates at his next words.

"Dakota and I are getting married. She'll be a Mayson." My jaw practically hits the floor when he turns to me and winks before adding. "Right, baby?"

Chapter Nine

Cooper

Dakota's fingernails dig into my skin as she stares at me with wide blue eyes. I give her hand a slight squeeze, and she blinks, her head tilting back to Kyra in confusion.

"Right." She seamlessly lets the mask fall firmly into place. "Married."

"Married?" Kyra gasps, her cheeks turning red.

"Yep." I bring Dakota's hand up to my lips and brush a kiss over her knuckles which has a gargled sound slipping past her lips.

"When?" Kyra blanches. "I haven't heard a single word about this."

"Don't think it's a secret. And to answer your question, this Saturday."

"You always said y'all were just friends." Kyra's tone rubs me the wrong way.

Just like her earlier comment about Dakota's last name.

"We were friends first." I drop our linked hands to rest on Dakota's toned thigh. "In my opinion, the best relationships are built on friendship. Wouldn't you agree?"

Kyra shifts in her chair. "I mean...yes. I just thought with your family..."

"My family has welcomed her with open arms, because she's one of the best people I've ever known. If you would have ever taken the time to see past the judgmental bullshit that this town spews, then you would know that."

My chest burns as I push to stand. "Thanks for the advice. But I would prefer to meet with your father next time."

Dakota stands abruptly, her lips still pressing in a firm line.

"A congrats would be nice," I toss out.

"Congrats," Kyra says with a scowl on her face.

"Thanks." I grin, then reach out to wrap my arm around Dakota's waist. "See you around, Kyra."

The truck door slams and I place one hand on the wheel, then drape the other over the back of Dakota's seat. I know what's coming.

"What in the actual fuck was that?"

There it is.

Dakota turns to face me, her dark hair framing her face. It never seizes to shock me at how beautiful she is. Naturally. She wore little makeup, and usually let her hair cascade down her back, long and wavy.

"Strategy," I respond bluntly.

She leans her head back on the headrest in frustration. "You do realize she's probably already on the phone telling everyone she knows that we're getting married?"

I lift a shoulder. "Let her."

"Cooper!" She shrieks. "Why the hell would you do that?"

"Think about it, Birdie." I reach out and take her hand. "You want custody. As much as it riles me the fuck up, people can be cruel, and the sins of your family have somehow been attached to you. I would do anything to erase that. To help you break free and to make sure you and Ari end up together."

Her eyes soften, and she squeezes my hand.

"I want to give you my name. You and Ari can live with me. Hell, I'm barely home. You would show you have a comfortable living arrangement. A stable income. Yours and mine. A family. A support system."

"And pity." She releases my hand. "I don't want your pity, Cooper. You of all people should know that."

"It's not pity." I grit my teeth. "You and I both know the chances of you gaining custody with a two person household is better than you being single."

She huffs, her hands flying up. "I know that, Cooper! But marriage is a big deal. A commitment."

"I'm fully aware of what marriage is." I adjust my position in my seat, the thought of what making Dakota my *wife* would actually intel.

Her having my name.

Her sleeping in my bed.

Her legs wrapped around my waist, as I slide....

Shit.

"Cooper." She nudges my arm.

"Sorry." I clear my throat.

"What about your family?"

"My family loves you," I point out.

"As you and your sister's friend. Not as a possible candidate for the mother of their future grandchildren."

I reach up and playfully tug a piece of her hair. "You already thinking about making pretty babies with me, Kota?"

She rolls her eyes. "Like you could handle me, cowboy."

I let a smirk trail over my lips. "Try me, sweetheart."

She narrows her eyes. "Can we please focus on the disaster at hand? The impromptu marriage that will be spreading all over town in the next ten minutes. Obviously, it's a little farfetched you'd choose me."

My jaw clenches at the offhand comment.

I'd always choose her.

"I don't know why you are freaking out," I say casually.

"Because you want us to galivant around being *fake married* in front of the entire town." Her head leans into her palm as she props her elbow up on the ledge of the window.

Nothing about marrying Dakota Sterling would be fake. *She just didn't need to know that. Yet.*

"What if they find out it's a lie?" She continues. "That we just staged this make believe family." She tosses her hands up. "What if they arrest me?"

"For what?" I chuckle.

"I don't know! Lying to a judge. Falsifying a marriage certificate. There has to be some kind of criminal consequences."

"The marriage would not be falsified. Not on paper. Not legally."

"It would have to look real. Like a real family." She runs a hand through her hair. "People would have to believe you would love me."

"Hey." I reach over and grip her chin between my fingers. "Any man would be lucky as hell to call you his wife. Understand me?"

"Sure," she mutters. I drop her chin as she continues. "We would have to give the illusion of a loving couple. Like a united front at parent teacher conferences and have things like health insurance, and a minivan." Her eyes widen. "I don't even have health insurance, and I can't pull a trailer with a minivan."

"Would you quit panicking?" My palm slides over to grip the nape of her neck. "Remember what I promised you?"

She sighs, her eyes fluttering closed as I knead her soft skin. "You know what this is?" I ask.

She opens her eyes. "What?"

"Me keeping my word." I squeeze. "Let me."

She stares at me, my heart thudding as I wait for her answer. I'm not sure why I'm nervous. It's not like she's marrying me for real. But honestly, I'll take Dakota Sterling any way I can have her.

"Ok," she finally whispers.

Thank God.

I dip my chin. "Ok."

She nods. "I guess we're getting married."

I crank the engine, then pull out, heading to the next stop.

"Where are we going?" She frowns.

I'm like a kid in a candy store.

"The courthouse."

"Cooper..."

The words are barely out of her mouth when both of our phone's start ringing.

I chuckle and flip on my blinker. "Well, that didn't take long."

Chapter Ten

Dakota

I stand at Cooper's kitchen island, nibbling my lip as his entire family congregates in the living room. I was able to talk him off of the ledge, and back to the ranch instead of the trip to the courthouse that would end in holy matrimony.

"Why are all of these people here?" Ari whispers, her eyes bouncing back and forth from me to the living room.

Ivy had taken her to town and gotten her a handful of things at the closest Wal-Mart while we were meeting with Norman. She has no idea what's happening and part of me wishes I could explain it to her first.

I watch Emmett, Cooper's dad that's been like a second father to me, and Ryder take a seat at the farmhouse table Cooper built.

Meanwhile, Ivy and Maddox speak in hushed voices to each other on the couch.

"We have news." Cooper appears behind me, tweaking my side.

"So we've heard." Maddox leans back, draping an arm around Ivy.

I elbow Cooper as Ruthie, his mother, a practical modern day angel on earth, flutters through the front door, followed by a frazzled Laiken.

"Gang is all here." Cooper claps his hands.

"Can someone explain what's going on?" Ruthie immediately crosses the room to my side. "Is this about Arizona?" Her eyes shine with concern.

Apparently, she's already been brought into the loop. I haven't had time to call and tell her about my sister, so I'm assuming Cooper filled her and Emmett in.

"Kind of?" I cringe.

Ruthie's arms wrap me in a warm hug. One that could only be given by a mother who loves her children more than life. I'd never been on the receiving end of one of those hugs growing up. Never had a mom that had an ounce of nurturing ability.

"We will do whatever it takes," she whispers.

Funny she says that.

"Can I have everyone's attention." Cooper coughs, his eyes latching onto mine as he pauses.

I give a subtle nod, my hands curling into tight fists.

This may be a bad idea.

"Dakota and I are getting married," he states.

Ruthie gasps, her hand coming up to land on her chest.

Ryder snorts, and Emmett looks completely unfazed.

"Not really married," I sputter out. "I mean like legally it's real but like." I motion my finger between me and the cowboy currently narrowing his eyes at me. "Like me and him. It's not real. It's fake."

"Fake." Ivy says the word slowly before blinking. "I'm really lost here."

"I offered to marry Dakota. To give her the Mayson name. Let's just say gaining custody of Arizona as a *Sterling* is going to be a challenge. She belongs with Kota. I want to make sure that happens."

At the admission, both Ruthie and Ivy's eyes fill with unshed tears. I feel emotion clog my throat, but I swallow it down. Suddenly I feel a hand on my arm. It's Laiken. Her soft and calming energy washes over me. You would think with her natural red locks she'd be all fire and sass, but she's the complete opposite.

"I'm not taking advantage of him. I'd never do that to your family. I promise." I clear my throat that's all of a sudden equivalent to the texture of sandpaper.

"Dakota," Ruthie scolds. "You know us better than that."

I want to wince at her expression. She looks hurt. "I will sign a prenup. Whatever needs to be done," I add.

"Not fucking happening," Cooper scoffs.

"I'd do one. You never know," Ryder tosses out from his spot at the table.

"You would you cynical bastard," Cooper grits out. "I trust Kota."

Ryder shakes his head but doesn't say more. To anyone else that would probably sting, but I give Ryder the benefit of the doubt. He's got his reasons.

"So, what do you need from us?" Ivy asks.

"We need you to play along." I sigh. "As far as everyone else in this town is concerned. I will be Cooper's wife."

Cooper crosses the room and flings an arm over my shoulder. "Dakota and Ari can live here. She'll have a stable home environment and a support system."

"Temporarily," I clarify. "Once I get full custody, we'll have a fall out. A realization that we were always better as friends and divorce. No harm no foul."

Even saying the words make my stomach churn.

"So basically, we need to be on alert if the court asks questions." Emmett leans his forearms on his knees. "You're a fine girl, Dakota. You work hard. Things will fall into place." Emmett glances around. "We're family. And we help our own. You need this." He shrugs. "We're here to support you."

Relief sweeps through me. Everyone seems to be on board. Everyone looks agreeable, but Ivy. I don't miss the concern painted across her face. I can see why. I just blindsided my best friend about marrying her brother.

"So how authentic are we going?" Ruthie grins. "It's not every day a woman's son gets married."

I laugh, my head shaking as Cooper drops his arm. "Nothing fancy for me. A courthouse and a document. That's all we need. Save the white gown and the sunset ceremony for when Cooper actually marries the love of his life."

I peer up at Cooper just in time to see him frown.

"Right," Ruthie says as she pushes to her feet. "Well, I guess there's only one thing left to say." Her smile is wide as she opens her arms. "Welcome to the family."

Chapter Eleven

Cooper

Thirteen Years Old

"Who you looking for?" Parker, my cousin asks as I crane my neck to peer around the cotton candy machine.

"Dakota." She's supposed to be meeting us here.

"That dark haired girl?" Parker grins. "She's pretty."

"Would you shut up?" I shove at his shoulder.

Dakota is pretty. Prettiest girl I ever saw, and it irritates me that he thinks so too. She moved here three years ago. I was shocked to see her at school that fall after I bought her those chips at the gas station, but we became fast friends. She loved horses and made me laugh.

"You like her." He studies my face before he shrugs. "It's cool, man."

I ignore him and start toward the hot dog stand where my sister Ivy, and my dad stand. The carnival comes to Mayson Ridge every fall for the harvest festival, and this is the first time Dakota has been able to come.

I'm just about to give up hope when I see her. Her long dark hair hangs over one shoulder as she walks cooly through the crowd.

"Kota!" I call, waving a hand.

Her smile widens, and her blue eyes brighten. She struts to us, and I don't miss how muddy her shoes are. I didn't see any mud on the way in here. Most of it dried out from the rain two nights ago.

"Sorry I'm late." She stops in front of us. "What are we riding first?"

"Dakota. Good to see you." My father steps over and gives her a hug.

"Hey, Mr. Mayson." She hugs him briefly before sliding back beside me.

"I told you to call me Emmett." He nudges her lightly. "You make me sound old."

That warrants a chuckle from me and Parker, because I hate to break it to him, but he's already old.

My gaze catches on the ride directly across from us.

"Ferris wheel?"

"Sounds good to me." She shrugs.

It's been two hours, and we've ridden every single ride. I even won her a stuffed bear that was almost as big as her.

"This was great, Coop." She grins up at the stars dotting the dark sky. "I want to come every year."

A scoff comes from beside me, and I turn to see Rhodes McDowell, and a few other guys from school approaching.

"I didn't think a Mayson would be slumming it." Rhodes slips a flask from his back pocket.

The fact he's fifteen and openly drinking at a county function shows just how stupid he really is.

"Excuse me?" I roll my shoulders back.

He lifts his chin in Dakota's direction. "Sterling, right?" He eyes Dakota. "On the wrong side of town ain't ya?"

I take a step forward, just as Parker places a palm on my chest.

"Fuck off, Rhodes." Parker shakes his head. "Leave her alone."

Rhodes gives Parker a light shove. "What are you going to do about it? Huh?"

Dakota's voice sails through the tension. "He ain't worth it, Parker."

Rhodes' gaze whips to Dakota, as her eyes remain hard and narrowed on him.

"Why don't you crawl back into the gutter you came from trailer trash," he sneers.

That was it.

My lungs burn, my pulse thrashes, and without a single ounce of hesitancy, I ball up my fist, and clock him right on the chin.

Rhodes falls to his back, wailing as my dad and a few other people come rushing over.

"What's going on here?" Dad barks.

"Nothing." He scrambles back, obviously not wanting to let on that he's been drinking. "We were just leaving."

My hand throbs as I shake it out, my rage still burning hot in my veins. But when a small, soft hand slides into mine, all that rage evaporates.

Dakota squeezes twice and my breathing slows.

"It's time to head out." My dad faces me. "Dakota, you got a ride?"

"Oh... yeah." She releases my hand and wraps her arms around the bear. "Y'all go ahead."

I reluctantly leave, my chest filled with an unfamiliar feeling. When we climb in the truck, my dad doesn't say much since Ivy and Parker are in the backseat. When he slows down just a few minutes down the road, I see a figure walking alone. Holding a stuffed bear.

My father rolls down his window.

"Dakota." His voice isn't angry, but it's strained. "Hop in."

She hesitates long enough to realize that he isn't leaving before she climbs in beside Ivy.

"Cute bear." Ivy smiles.

"Thanks. Muscles up there won it for me."

Her tone is light. Like her walking home in the dark is completely normal.

"What's your address, Dakota?"

When I peer over my shoulder, her face pales before she snaps out of it. "You can just drop me at the corner of First and Holloway."

My father nods, but he doesn't speak. When we get to the intersection, he doesn't stop, he turns right, heading into the Mayson Ridge Mobile Home Park.

"Which house?" He asks.

Dakota lets out a sigh before she mutters. "Fifth one on the right."

When we pull into the drive, my stomach clenches. I knew she lived in a trailer. But this....

"Thanks. See you at school, Coop." She jumps out, running up the broken steps before quietly slipping inside the dingy trailer door.

It finally hit me.

She walked all the way to that carnival. That's why her shoes were muddy.

Chapter Twelve

Dakota

"I'm kind of confused." Arizona stands behind me in Cooper's bedroom, eyeing me in the full length mirror.

"About what?" I adjust the sleeve of my dress.

The dress that I just had to pilfer through three plastic tubs in my horse trailer to find.

I finally moved most of my things to Cooper's cabin last night, and to say I'm losing my shit would be an excellent description. *I'm getting married today. To Cooper Mayson.*

"You and Cooper." She rolls her eyes before she steps up to me, tucking in the tag of my dress.

"What about me and Cooper?" I reach for my cowboy boots, then drop down on the bed to slip them on.

"I thought y'all were like a thing." Her right eyebrow raises.

"A thing?"

"Dating. Courting. Whatever you old people are calling it these days."

I burst out a laugh. "We're friends."

"That's a crock," she scoffs. "And a big fat lie."

"Arizona!" I push to stand. "We have never crossed the friendship line. It's firmly in place."

"Why not?"

"Because. It's not like that." I huff, flipping my hair back off of my shoulders.

I'm already sweating.

"I mean, I wouldn't blame you. Cooper is a baddie."

"A what?"

"Baddie. Bad. Hot." She throws her hands up. "I'm going to get on my good clothes. The ones with the fringe. Feels very on fleek for this occasion."

I snort, almost not believing how alike we are. The look on her face when Ruthie brought her that fringe skirt had me nearly peeing my pants. Ari looked horrified.

I smooth my hands over my white sundress just as Ivy pokes her head in. "Knock knock."

"Hey." I twirl around. "Well, for a fake bride, how do I look?"

She smiles, but her eyes don't twinkle like normal.

"Are you ok?" I cross the room. "I know this is a lot, Ives. And I'm sorry I didn't come to you with it first. It just happened so fast."

She shakes her head. "I'm not upset, Dakota." She sighs, her hands gripping mine. "I'm worried."

"About what?" I furrow my brow.

"You and Coop," she admits. "Your friendship."

I relax a fraction. "Nothing could ruin our friendship. That's the whole reason he's doing this."

"I know." She nods, then squeezes my hands. "I just don't want either of you to get hurt."

"We won't. Plus, we will have solid rules." I drop her hands. "Like a contract. Simple."

"Simple." She chuckles. "You are anything but simple, Dakota Sterling."

I stick my tongue out. "And that's why I'm your favorite."

She laughs, her head tilting back. "You are one of a kind." Her expression turns solemn. "And I would love nothing more than for you to be my sister."

"It's fake, Ives," I remind her.

"Is it?" She tilts her head.

"There she is!" Ruthie's voice interrupts our conversation, just in time for me to avoid admitting the secret that I've been harboring for over half of my life.

"I'm ready." I hold my arms out.

"You look beautiful." She grins, her blonde hair in soft waves.

She looks so much like Ivy when she wears her hair down.

"Now, I know you two don't want a big fuss, but I did bring over something old, and something borrowed."

"Ruthie," I scold.

"Oh, stop it." She twirls her finger. "This is an old necklace my mother gave me on my twenty first birthday, and these earrings are my favorite pearls you can borrow."

I hold back the emotion as she clasps the necklace around my neck.

"Thank you," I whisper.

"You have something new and blue?" Ivy asks.

"My panties." I grin.

"Gross." Ivy gags.

"Alright. We have thirty minutes to get to the courthouse. Emmett, Ryder, and Cooper will meet us there. Where is Ari?"

"Present." Ari slips down the hall; her fringe skirt paired with a cream long sleeve shirt.

Ruthie gasps, her hand flying to her mouth. "What a beauty."

"I prefer the term *baddie,* but beauty will do," Ari says casually.

Ivy giggles and I roll my eyes.

"Come on you little baddie." I wink. "Let's go find my groom."

Chapter Thirteen

Cooper

“She’s late,” I grumble.

“Did you expect anything less?” My father chuckles. “That girl will be late to her own funeral.”

“Can we not talk about her dying.” I eye him, tugging at the silver chain around my neck.

For some reason I’m nervous. Like she might change her mind and run. Try to handle this on her own like she does most things.

Like changing three tires on a trailer in the middle of the night coming back from San Antonio. Or like when she tried to put the fire out at the farmhouse with just a flimsy garden hose. I’d never been so fucking scared in my entire life when I saw her running toward those flames. Trying to save *my* family home.

I blow out a breath, my pulse jumping when the doors to the courthouse open. My mother leads the group, then she steps aside, holding the door open with a bright smile. Ivy enters first, followed by Ari, and then....my *girl.*

Dakota enters the room, a short white sundress hitting mid thigh. Her tan legs are visible, but barely because a pair of turquoise cowboy boots hit just below her knee. Her long dark hair is in lose curls, and her lips are painted a soft pink.

Her smile grows when she struts to me. "You ready to do this, cowboy?"

My neck feels hot. My shoulders tense.

She's absolutely stunning. Ryder slaps me on the back, so I clear my throat and turn on the typical Cooper charm

"Ready and willing, darlin." I hold out my elbow.

The banter has always been easy between us. Natural. Sometimes flirty, but never beyond a simple tease. She may think I'm kidding most of the time, but truth is, I'm not.

"Right here." I open a mahogany door, leading us into the office, leaving the rest of my family to wait in the area of the courthouse designated for marriages. We had already gotten our license earlier this week, we just needed the officiating to make it legit.

I approach the counter, smiling at the woman in her late sixties. "Cooper Mayson and Dakota Sterling."

She eyes me through her glasses. "Well didn't you turn into a handsome young man."

I give a lopsided smile. "Thanks, Trudy."

She picks up her desk phone. "Let me just call Ernie."

Dakota and I stand at the counter as she talks to Ernie in a hushed tone that she thinks we can't hear.

"Yeah. The Mayson boy." She pauses. "No, not the mean one." She glances over at us. "And he's marrying that *girl.*"

She holds her hand over the phone, pulling it way from her mouth. "You can head into room three, hon. Ernie will meet you in there. You got a witness, right?"

"Yes ma'am." I nod.

"Wow," Dakota says as we leave the office. "That *girl.* That's actually one of the kinder descriptions I've had."

"Well Trudy is no innocent herself. It's been rumored she gets sticky fingers during tithing on Sundays."

"No way." Dakota snickers. "Scandalous."

I motion a hand to the small group we have now hovering in the waiting area. Maddox, Laiken, and her son Trace have now joined.

"Dakota!" Trace shrieks.

Dakota crouches down, her arms open as he launches himself at her. "You look reallllly pretty."

"Aren't you the sweetest." She presses a kiss to his forehead. "You wrangle any horses without me?"

"No." He leans back and pouts. "Mom won't let me. She says six years old is too *young* to be by myself."

"Well, she's kind of right." Dakota tickles his sides. "Plus. I need my partner in crime." He giggles as Laiken steps forward.

"Alright buddy. Let's get inside."

"Y'all go ahead." I hold open the door as everyone files in, leaving me and Dakota alone in the hallway.

She watches me, her posture a little tense. "You ready for this?"

She nods, her hands wringing together. "I think so."

Reaching for her hand, I intertwine her fingers with mine. "Keeping my word."

With a deep breath we enter into the room, slowly walking toward Ernie who stands at a podium. Once we make it to the hypothetical altar, he gives us both a quick glance before he begins the process.

"Join hands please," he instructs.

I face Dakota, taking her hands in mine. I can tell she's anxious, so I slide my thumbs back and forth in a rhythmic motion. I'm not really paying much attention to Ernie. I'm focused on those beautiful blue eyes. Those perfect lips.

"Cooper, it's time for your vows. Repeat after me." Ernie holds up a hand, but I interrupt.

"Actually, Ernie. I'd like to say my own vows." I meet his eyes before moving mine back to Dakota.

She looks panicked. "Cooper. I didn't..." she whispers but I shake my head.

"I wanted to do this."

I spent all night thinking about this. If this was my only chance to be her husband, I was going to be the best one she ever had. And I may never get the chance to tell her how I feel. Not really.

Ernie gives me the go ahead, so I let mine and Dakota's eyes latch onto each other again.

"Kota, I vow to always see you. To protect you when you feel vulnerable. To listen to you when you need your voice, and to believe in you when you can't find the strength to believe in yourself. I vow to always be your safe place. To be your best friend, and to love you with no conditions. No boundaries and no expectations. I might not always be perfect, but I sure as shit will never stop trying to be for you."

Chuckles filter through the room followed by Trace's small voice whispering *he said a bad word.*

When I finish, Dakota's eyes glisten as she swallows thickly. Her thumbs swipe in tandem with mine, brushing the side of my palms.

Ernie glances at Dakota. "Dakota, your vows."

She opens her mouth, but closes it when a tear leaks down her cheek. Inhaling deeply, she manages to grab a hold of her voice.

"What he said," she croaks out.

More chuckles echo through the room again, and Dakota lets out a laugh mingled with a quiet sob. I can't contain my own laugh as my shoulder shake slightly.

"Well, Dakota. Do you take this man to be your husband?" Ernie asks.

She stares at me, a smile tugging at her lips. "I do."

"Cooper, do you take Dakota to be your wife?" Ernie addresses me.

"I do," I answer.

"Do you have the rings?" He asks.

Dakota's face falls again, realizing the rings are something we didn't discuss. But I always knew the kind of ring I'd get her one day.

"Sure do." I reach in my pocket, pulling out the two circular bands.

She narrows her eyes at me, obviously seeing that I went rogue.

Of course I went rogue.

I hold out my hand to Dakota. The simple silver band is etched with a saddle pattern. She holds it in her palm, while Ernie motions to me.

"Dakota. Please place the ring on Cooper's finger."

I hold out my left hand as her trembling fingers slide the ring on easily.

I catch her fingers, squeezing her hand lightly before she drops it by her side.

"Cooper. Your ring for Dakota."

I hold up the princess cut diamond that's mounted on a matching silver band like mine. It's a little thicker, the edges decorated in tiny diamond that sparkle in the light.

"Cooper," Dakota gasps softly.

I take her hand in mine, slipping the ring over her delicate finger. It fits perfect.

Looks perfect.

Her. Wearing *my* ring.

"By the power vested in me by the great state of Texas, I now pronounce you husband and wife. You may kiss your bride."

Dakota's eyes widen, as if she had completely forgotten this crucial part of the tradition. But I didn't forget. I drop her hand, letting my palm lift to slide beneath her hair and around the nape of her neck. Then I do something I've wanted to since I was thirteen years old. I kiss her.

Chapter Fourteen

Dakota

Oh. My. God.

Cooper Mayson was kissing me.

Like actually kissing me.

His rough palm tugs slightly against my neck, his lips melting against mine like we'd been kissing for years. I was startled, in shock, and completely at his mercy. A low groan filters from his mouth as he opens, coaxing me to do the same. My lips move hypnotically against his, before feeling his tongue slowly slide inside of my mouth, licking a flame of heat up my spine. His free hand pulls me flush against his broad frame, and my hands involuntarily curl into his pearl snap. Another soft stroke of his tongue has a gasp traveling between us, because in my twenty-five years I'd never kissed a pair of lips that made me feel like *this.* Which was dangerous. Because Cooper Mayson was my best friend. And as of approximately a minute and a half ago, my *fake* husband.

When he gently pecks me on my tingling lips, I open my eyes. He smirks, while I stand there like a lust drunk lunatic.

The room, which I'm remembering houses his entire family, is completely silent. Not a single sound, until someone finally breaks the tension, a whistle howling from somewhere in the room, followed by claps and cheers.

Cooper moves as if he's unfazed, snatching my hand in his before he's dragging us out to his family that carry huge smiles on their faces. I feel like a fumbling mess. My legs are like jelly, and my stomach is wound tighter than a barrel racer's jeans.

"Congratulations!" Ruthie grips me in a hug, followed by Emmett and Ivy.

I hug them quickly, trying not to give anything away about my current emotional state.

Which considering my first kiss with the man I've loved since childhood was in front of his own mother and father means I'm venturing into 2007 Brittany territory. I smile while Ruthie snaps a few photos before I excuse myself to the bathroom. Inside the safety of the public restroom, I check my face. My skin is flushed, my lips pouty from the kiss, and my pupils are blown. Geez.

I close my eyes, reeling myself back to reality. This is Cooper. *My Cooper.* All sunshine and cowboy boots. The flirt. He was putting on a show. Glancing down at my hand, I stare at the beautiful diamond on my finger. It's the most beautiful ring I've ever seen.

It's fictional, Dakota. Nothing more.

I take another deep breath as I remind myself, he's playing the role. Cooper never did anything half ass, so I would expect nothing less in his role as my husband. I just hope I can keep the two separate. Which reminds me. Those rules need to be discussed, stat. Because now I was certain, *kissing* was definitely off of the table. Effective immediately.

When I leave the restroom, I almost collide into a strong wall of muscle. Cooper's hands land on my shoulders, steadying me on my boots.

"Hey, you good?"

"Oh, yeah." I wave a hand. "I'm fine. Needed to pee," I lie.

He squints at me before using his thumb to swipe a spot next to my bottom lip. "You got some lipstick here," he says, his voice husky. "Sorry if I surprised you. I thought the kiss would be a nice touch." His lip tilts up at the corner, and I will my heart to quit fluttering.

It's getting ridiculous.

I revert back to our typical back and forth, aiming for normal. "I was impressed. Glad I could confirm that Mariann Smith wasn't lying," I quip.

Mariann Smith was Cooper's first kiss at the homecoming in the seventh grade. She came into the girl's bathroom at the football game gushing about what a good kisser he was.

I cried for three days.

"Well for the record, you're a hell of a lot better kisser than Mariann Smith." He peers down at me, his eyes dropping to my mouth.

"Practice makes perfect." I smile.

His smile falters briefly, and I would have missed it if I didn't know him so well.

"And the rings. Nice save," I add.

He steps closer. "You think I'd marry you without a ring?"

I gape up at him. "You probably spent way too much money on this, Cooper."

"Like I'd let my wife walk around with anything less than the best."

My cheeks heat, the word *wife* sounding so natural coming from his lips.

I open my mouth to respond when we're interrupted.

"Hey, guys." Ivy peeks around the corner. "We're going to take Trace and Ari for ice cream. Why don't y'all take the afternoon to get settled at the house and I will bring her by in a few hours."

My heart warms. "She would love that. Thank you."

Ivy waves and I look back at Coop. "Ready to head home, Mr. Mayson?"

He offers me his elbow. "You bet, Mrs. Mayson."

Mrs. Mayson.

I like the sound of that.

Maybe too much.

Chapter Fifteen

Cooper

I glance down to the sheet of notebook paper in my hand before I look back up at Dakota who's sitting cross legged on the couch. She changed into those fucking yoga pants that show off her shapely ass and I've yet to forget how her tongue felt against mine less than two hours ago. So, focusing is a challenge at the moment.

"What exactly is this?" I ask, tossing down the paper with a list of *rules* halfway down the page.

After she brought the last of her things from the trailer, she must have conjured this list while I was in the barn checking the horses.

"Our marriage rules." She picks it up. "You know, to keep things in line."

I narrow my eyes. "Ok......"

She holds up a finger. "Number one on the list. I will pay a monthly rent."

"No," I say instantly.

She lifts a brow. "Excuse me?"

"I said no. My *wife* will not pay *me* rent to live in *our* house."

"Cooper," she grits out.

"This is not up for discussion," I fire back, relaxing into the oversized chair.

"Ok fine. But I will contribute to the household. I can pay the utility bills."

"We have well water." I hold up a hand as she begins to argue. "You want to contribute? You can focus your time on Ari. Contribute to making her feel welcome and comfortable."

She stares at me for a moment before clearing her throat. "Fine. Number two." She points her blue eyes at me. "I will not crowd your space or take over your room. I can sleep on the couch, while Ari makes the guest room hers."

"No."

She slams the paper down on the sofa. "You can't just say no to every rule."

"Oh, I can, Birdie." I grin. "We're a team. Meaning, we make decisions together."

"Why can't I sleep on the couch?" She asks, crossing her arms.

"Because I'm not making you sleep on a couch while I'm in a warm bed," I scoff.

"I'm not kicking you out of your bed, Cooper." She rolls her eyes. "That's inconsiderate."

"You're right. You're not." I lean forward, planting my elbows on my knees. "You'll sleep with me."

Her shoulders go ridged. "Yeah, no."

"We've slept together before." I shrug. "It's no different than when we were kids."

Lie. It's totally fucking different. She knows it and I know it. But I want her next to me. Period.

"And if memory serves me correctly, you're a total cover hog."

"I think you are mistaken. It's you who always rolled up like a tortilla. I nearly got frostbite that Christmas."

She laughs, her hands flying to her face before she shakes her head. "Ok then. We can share a bed."

"Good."

"On one condition. I get my own comforter."

"Done," I agree.

"Number three." She holds up three fingers.

"How many rules do you have?" I ask.

"Just a few more." She picks the paper back up. "Number three. I understand we need to show some PDA. Being married means affection is normal." She hesitates before she shifts on the couch. "I think holding hands and a quick peck on the lips is fine in public." She lifts a brow at me. "No tongue."

"Why not?" I smirk.

She squirms again.

Oh, she liked the tongue.

"I don't think it's necessary." She points at me. "You snuck it on me today."

"Like you didn't enjoy it." I wag my brows.

"Oh stop," she scoffs. "I'm not backing down on this one. No tongue."

"In public. Got it." I nod.

She said nothing about in private.

"Which leads me to number four." She moves to place her feet flat on the floor. "I understand you have.... needs. I don't expect you to be celibate for however long this takes. It could be months. If you feel the need to...get female attention. Do it away from Mayson Ridge. Last thing we need is rumors of you having an affair one month into the marriage."

For some reason that last rule just pisses me straight off. Not only at the fact she thinks I would sleep with another woman while married to her, but that she might want to sleep with another man.

Not fucking happening.

"Let me be clear on this, Kota." I push to my feet, staring down at her. "While my ring is on your finger, and my last name attached to yours, there will not be any other women. Period."

She gulps, her eyes widening. "Coop..."

I lean down, gripping her chin between my fingers. "And there will be no other men while you are *my* wife. Understood?"

Her jaw slacks, before she nods. "Understood."

"Alright. I need to run an errand. I'll be back." I drop a kiss on her head, before striding to the door.

When I make it to my truck, I blow out a breath before cranking the engine. I've got my work cut out for me. I may have had an ulterior motive for marrying Dakota Sterling. Yes, I want her to get custody, but I also want to prove to her that she doesn't have to be afraid to let go anymore. I've got only a handful of months to prove to the woman I love that she's right where she was always meant to be. *With me.*

Chapter Sixteen

Dakota

A knock sounds at the door, breaking my spiraling thoughts. I've been folding my clothes in Cooper's room for the last thirty minutes. After he left, I got busy. The less time I spent thinking about the kiss that altered my brain chemistry and the fact that he wants me to sleep next to him every night the better off I'll be.

I remind myself that this is for Ari. I can do this for her. He hasn't made a move on me in fifteen years. He's not going to start now. Not like I would accept it anyway. His friendship means too much to me, and at some point, I'd let him down. His family down, and there just wasn't a part of me that could chance it. Not with my track record.

I drop one of my favorite hoodies before I hustle to the door.

"It's us!" Ivy calls as she steps in.

"How was ice cream?" I ask as Ari walks farther into the room.

"Fire." She says before heading to the hallway. "Thanks, Ivy." She looks to me. "Is it ok if I go back here and draw?"

"Sure."

I make a mental note to get her more supplies. I've seen her doodling in a notepad all week.

When she disappears down the hall, I peer over at Ivy. "Fire?"

"It means good," she offers. "I had to ask too."

I chuckle, moving to the kitchen. "Thank you for taking her. Need anything to drink?"

"I'm good. Maddox is waiting in the truck." She taps her fingers on the island, hovering next to a barstool.

"Ivy." I brace a hand on the counter. "Spit it out."

"He kissed you," she blurts.

"Was it that obvious?" I tease.

She laughs. "I thought he was going to swallow your face."

I feign annoyance. "He thought it was *a nice touch.*"

"It was a touch alright," she quips.

I reach for a dirty cup in the sink, trying to keep myself from blushing. "You know Coop. He takes his roles seriously. Remember when he was Peter Pan in the high school play?"

"Oh my God." She leans her head back on a laugh. "Ryder never let him live those green tights down."

"Neither did I." I grin.

Her smile fades, and her eyes turn soft. "You know, it wouldn't be so bad if this was.... real."

I freeze, my hands resting under the cold faucet. "Ivy...."

She lifts her palms. "I'm not meddling. I just want you both to be happy. And if this is something that would make you happy...."

I flip off the faucet. "You know I love him. He's always been there for me, but I'm not...." I pause, trying to put how I feel into words. "He deserves the best."

She tilts her head to the side. "And what makes you think you aren't?"

My phone buzzes on the counter, dragging my attention away for a split second. When I see the name flashing across the screen, my entire body stills.

Bzzzz.Bzzz.

I blink, my vision growing blurry. I know I shouldn't answer. I know he doesn't deserve my time. My breath. But there's always that little voice in my head. That voice that guilts me into picking up the phone. Guilt that eats at my soul. *He's in there because of you.*

My shaky hand reaches for my cell, my pulse thudding as I hit accept. The recorded voice comes on the other end of the line. *You have a collect call from Cove County Correctional Facility from* Billy Sterling. *Press one to accept.*

I grip the edge of the counter, while Ivy moves quickly toward me, her expression worried.

I bring the phone down, pressing the number *one* with an unsteady hand. Lifting it back to my ear, I hold my breath.

"Dakota." His voice flows through the phone, the tone just as berating as it's always been.

"Billy," I grind out.

"Got good news." He chuckles, the rasp causing my skin to crawl. "Daddy's coming home."

And just like that, when I thought everything would be falling into place, suddenly, it was falling apart.

Chapter Seventeen

Cooper

Sixteen Years Old

The buzzer that sounds through the arena indicates the end of the ride. The bare back event just started, which meant Dakota was late. I scan the crowd from our seat in the bleachers, looking for long legs and a contagious smile. She was supposed to be catching a ride with Laiken and considering Laiken is already here, I'm assuming it didn't pan out.

I lean forward to see around Maddox and Ryder.

"Where's Kota?" I call out to Laiken.

She frowns. "I don't know. I called her three times. She never came outside. I figured maybe she hitched a ride with someone else."

My sister glances up at me, her eyes unsure as Brady, her boyfriend tosses an arm over her shoulder.

"She's probably just being Dakota. Running around here on someone's horse." He chuckles.

Could be. Dakota had a way with horses. Since the first time she rode one at the ranch, you couldn't keep her off of one.

I fish out my cell, dialing her number as they announce the next rider. It rings until I get her voicemail. I curse under my breath, but thumb over to her contact and click on her location. Her asshole father wouldn't get her a phone, so I talked to my parents about adding another line. It was only fifteen dollars a month, so I pay for it out of my paycheck I get from working at the ranch each week. I wanted her to have a way to reach me when shit got bad. Billy Sterling was a mean drunk, and a low class criminal who already had one too many DUI's, and even an assault charge. She's called me more than once to pick her up when he was on one of his benders and for some reason, something in my gut wasn't sitting right. Because the marker on my maps indicated where she was. Mayson Ridge Mobile Home Park.

"I'll be back." I push to my feet.

"Where you going?" Ryder asks, his eyes focused on the horse bucking toward the fence line.

"Something is off. Going to get Kota," I say before shoving my phone back in my pocket.

Ryder glances up at me, his expression turning to stone. "Need me to come?"

I shake my head. "That's ok, I got her."

All of my family is aware of her situation, and she's quickly becoming not just my best friend, but a part of the family.

Hurrying down the sea of bleachers filled with cowboy hats and teenagers sneaking vodka in their Styrofoam cups, I make a beeline for my truck then peel out of the rodeo grounds, unease settling in my chest.

When I pull up to the trailer with the warping paint and rotted skirting, I slam my truck in park and jump out. I notice Billy's truck is gone and part of me is relieved because I've come close to beating his ass more than once, and tonight, I'm not sure I can hold back any longer. I hate this feeling of anxiety. The fear he's finally crossed a line. My fist pounds on the door, my voice loud as I holler for Dakota. After knocking once more, I reach for the knob, twisting it easily before I step inside. The stench of smoke hits me first, the thick fog causing my eyes to burn. Empty beer cans are scattered across the living room, along with three different ashtrays filled to the brim with old buds of cigarettes. I've never been inside before, and the sheer filth has me grinding my molars.

"Kota," I call.

The stale atmosphere has me cracking my neck, my hands flexing as I stride through the trailer, strategically moving around the trash and dirty piles of clothes. There's a room at the end of the hall, the light dimly shining from beneath the crack of the door.

"Birdie," I call, opening the door with caution.

The room is the only one in the house free of smoke. It smells like spice and leather, a familiar scent that I know is my cologne. A lone bottle sits on the window sill, one she must have taken from my room.

My heart aches.

Fuck, Kota.

The room is spotless. A twin mattress sits flush on the faded green carpet, made up with two small, yellow pillows. And the bear. The one that I won for her at our first carnival. Three tubs line the back wall, along with two pairs of boots.

The ones I bought her.

My teeth grit as anger rises. She doesn't even have a fucking bed or dresser.

I'm about to walk back out into the hallway, when I hear a small sound coming from the closet in the corner. My feet move quick, my boots heavy as I cross the room before opening the broken door with a crack zigzagging right down the middle. Nothing could have prepared me for what I saw.

A lump lodges in my throat as misty blue eyes meet mine. They shine with tears, along with a nasty bruise forming under her left eye. Dried blood scatters across her lip, the corner busted as she sits curled up in a ball in the floor of the closet.

Motherfucker.

"Coop," she sobs out.

Dropping to my knees, I reach out my arms, inviting her into my safety. She climbs up from the floor, her arms wrapping around my neck as she sobs into my shoulder.

Fire ignites in my veins, anger and rage boiling as she squeezes me tighter.

"Sshhh. I'm here," I whisper, my hold strong. "I'm so sorry, Kota. I'm here."

I knew two things for sure. One, I hate Billy Sterling. And two, he's never going to lay a hand on her again.

I hold Dakota's hand tightly in mine as we walk inside the front door of my house. My father is sitting in the recliner, my mother in the kitchen. When the door shuts, he glances back at me and frowns.

"I figured y'all would still be at the rode...." His voice trails off, his body lifting from the chair when he sees Dakota's face. "Ruthie."

My mom comes fluttering from the kitchen, wiping her hands on her apron as she smiles. But it falls the second she lands her eyes on us.

"Oh, sweetheart," she says, her eyes misting over.

Dakota squeezes my hand. I can barely speak.

"Why don't you let Ruthie clean you up and get you something to drink?" My father's voice is soft as he looks from my mom to Dakota.

I squeeze her hand back, and she quietly swipes a tear from her eye. "Thank you."

I don't what to let her go. I want to hold her hand forever. Protect her from that monster. But I do as my dad said and watch with agony as she lets my mom wrap her up in a hug while silent sobs wrack her body.

The lump in my throat grows, the rage returning. I feel a heavy palm on my shoulder.

"Keys."

I blink and look over to him. "What?"

"Your keys." He locks eyes with me. "I know what you want to do son, and you won't be any use to her if you act on it."

Tears spring in my eyes as I hesitate before pulling my keys out from my pocket. I place them in his hand just as his palm squeezes my shoulder.

"It's ok," he says quietly.

I feel the tears stream down my face, my nose burning. He shoves my keys in his pocket, his eyes locking with mine again.

I finally manage to speak. "Can she stay?"

He dips his chin. "As long as she needs to."

Chapter Eighteen

Dakota

"Kota." Ivy's hand lands on my shoulder, bringing me back to the moment.

The terrifying moment that my worst fear was spoken into existence.

I drop my cell, my eyes darting to hers.

"It was your dad?" She runs her hands up and down my arms.

"He's...."

Said he was coming *home.* He's being released? Why?

"He said he's coming home," I whisper.

Her eyes widen before she reaches for her own phone. "I'll tell Maddox he can go to the cabin. I'll stay with..."

"No." I shake my head. "I'm ok."

Lie.

Billy was probably lying. Trying to scare me. I never could trust a word coming out of his mouth.

"Are you sure? Cooper isn't home yet, and I don't want you to..."

Be impulsive. Reckless.

As usual.

On any other day I would. But I have a twelve year old girl down the hall who needs me to be in control.

"Seriously, Ivy. I'm alright."

I'll break down later.

She studies me a second before she slides her phone back into her pocket. "Ok."

"I need to check on Arizona anyway. I'm sure she's wondering what the plan is from here. That's what we should focus on."

With a quick nod, she wraps me in a hug. "I'm here if you need me."

"Thanks, Ives."

Once the front door shuts behind her, I take a deep breath.

He can't hurt you.

He's far away.

He won't come back here.

My palms land on the countertop as I close my eyes. The urge to run is strong. The urge to ride. To hideout. But it was time I stopped letting Billy Sterling wreak havoc on my life. Even from behind bars.

Moving my feet, I start down the hallway, stopping in front of the guest bedroom door. I knock twice, waiting for Arizona to respond.

"Come in," she calls.

I crack open the door, peeking in. "You got a sec?"

She sits her notepad down on the bed. "Step into my office."

This girl has such a personality.

Pushing my way through the door, I make it to the bed, sitting down on the end while she's resting against the headboard.

"So, how are you doing?" I ask, wincing when she keeps a blank stare.

"Fine." She fidgets with her pencil. "Are you ok?"

"Me? Of course." I pull my legs up, tucking them beneath me. "I just wanted to make sure you were settling in. See if there was anything you needed. I'm sure you are wondering what the heck is going on around here."

"I'm good. I actually have a bed to sleep in, so no complaints here." She shrugs.

My heart pangs. Then anger rises at my mother. How careless she was.

"Well, you will always have a bed to sleep in here. I promise you," I tell her with sincerity.

"Now that Cooper and I are legally married, we can file the paperwork to request custody. It will most likely be temporary at first, and we have to jump through a few hoops, but I don't want you to worry."

"Ok." She flickers her eyes up to me.

"And we need to get you into school soon. What are you in, sixth or seventh grade?"

"I was in seventh in New Orleans. But it's not like I was there all that often."

I frown. "What do you mean?"

"Bea wasn't an early riser." She tucks a piece of her dark hair behind her ear. "She wouldn't wake up in time to take me, and it was a really long walk. The area wasn't very good, and I wasn't about to end up on some random missing flyer in the Seven Eleven."

"Who took you to school?" I curl my hands into fists.

If Bea was still alive, this is about the time I'd be paying her a visit.

"Sometimes I took the bus. Or sometimes she would take me if she never went to sleep the night before." Her expression is flat as she relays the formation.

Like it's normal.

I remember the first time I really understood what was happening at my house wasn't *normal.* Not until I met the Mayson's, did I realize what a loving family really looked like.

"I'm really sorry, Arizona." I meet her eyes. "It wasn't fair."

"Life isn't fair. Right?" She picks up her pencil, going back to her drawing.

I watch her hunched shoulders loosen when she starts scribbling. Her pencil moves in steady strokes as she lets out her feelings through the lead.

This is her outlet. Her peace. Just like horses are mine.

"Ok. I'll let you get some rest. Dinner will be ready in an hour or so. Tomorrow, I have to work, but it's just here at the ranch for a few hours. You are welcome to come out to the arena and watch."

She nods. "Ok."

Sensing she needs time alone, I climb off the bed, glancing back to the clothes she has piled neatly in the corner of the room. She hasn't even put them in the dresser. Another pang slashes across my chest.

She's never had a home. And I was determined more than ever to give her one.

Closing the door behind me, I quietly slip down the hall and back to the kitchen. I had just made it to the island when the front door flew open and Cooper stormed in. His eyes were wild, his chest heaving.

He was in front of me in three strides, tossing his hat onto the counter with narrowed eyes before asking, "What did that motherfucker want?"

Chapter Nineteen

Cooper

"Thanks for putting a rush on those, Wade." I reach out to shake his hand.

He takes it with a firm grip before dropping it.

"What's the damage?" I pull out my wallet.

Wade was one of the best custom jewelers in town. He wasn't here yesterday when I picked up the rings, and his wife just told me to come by tomorrow and sort it out. She wanted to be sure we had them at the ceremony.

"Consider it a wedding gift." He nods.

Wade was a master at hand made silver. He did everything from jewelry to buckles to custom spurs.

"Let me pay you," I insist.

"Nope. Anita and I have known you both since you were kids." He crosses his arms. "And it's about damn time anyway."

I lift a brow.

"Don't think you were so slick, son." He shakes his head. "You've been chasing that girl for years."

Ain't that the truth.

"Congrats, Cooper."

"Thanks, Wade." I give him a hug with a slap on the back before climbing into the seat of my truck.

Cranking the engine, I shift in drive when my phone rings.

Ivy.

I tap the phone icon on the screen. "Hey Ives."

"Hey."

"What's up?"

"Where are you?" Her voice changes and I immediately tense.

"Why? What's wrong?" I place my hands on the wheel, my fingers flexing.

"Dakota got a call."

My hands clench. "What did he want?"

"I don't really know, she was kind of in shock. She assured me she was fine, but I think you need to get there."

I curse under my breath. "I'm on my way."

By the time I make it to the ranch, my heart rate is through the roof. Every time he calls it was like she took five steps back. Completely undid all the progress she's made. Her dad would guilt her, manipulate her, and have her so screwed up it usually took me a couple of days to rid the *Billy* from her mindset.

Slamming my truck in drive, I park in front of the cabin. My heart pounds when I jump out, then march up the stairs.

The door is unlocked, which pisses me off even more. Not that anyone could get to her or Arizona, but it's different now. *They're my responsibility.*

Dakota stands at the kitchen island when I come through the door, her eyes wide. I cross the room, tossing my cowboy hat onto the counter.

"What did that motherfucker want?" I grit out.

"Ivy called you?"

"Don't deflect. Tell me."

Her hands slide down the side of her legs. "He said...." She shakes her hands out. "He said he's coming home."

I freeze. My boots glued to the floor.

"Coming home?" I question.

"He didn't give any details. Just that condescending tone he always has. Even referred to himself as *daddy*," she scoffs.

I watch her closely. "You, ok?"

"Fine."

"Kota."

"Coop," she repeats, turning to face the stove.

"It's me." I remind her.

She places her hands on the counter, her chin dropping.

Not giving a fuck about rules or boundaries, I slide my arm around her waist and tug her back to my front. I lean down, burying my face in her neck. "It's just me, Birdie."

I feel her breath hitch, then her body sags against me. "I can't break, Coop. Ari is here. I'm fine. Who knows if he's even telling the truth."

I close my eyes, breathing her in for the few seconds she allows me to before she pulls away.

"I can make some calls." I watch her grab a pot from under the sink.

A part of me loves that she knows where everything is already. That she's so comfortable in my home.

"They are required to notify me if he gets released." She drops the pot on the counter. "I guess we just wait and see."

Wait and see.

I should have ended Billy Sterling years ago, but this time is different. I'm not some young kid with a hot head. I'm her *husband.* And I protect what's mine.

Chapter Twenty

Dakota

"Thank you for supper." Arizona picks up her plate. "Those wings were sick."

Cooper lifts a brow.

"Sick. As in good." She shakes her head. "Do I need to make you a glossary?"

I laugh at the way these two have bantered all evening. With the event filled day, first a wedding to the man I'm pretending not to love, and then the man I loathe more than anything on this planet possibly being released from prison, I needed a light moment. A moment to let Ari fill the air with her quick wit and impressive wealth of alligator facts.

"You're welcome." I push to my feet, reaching to pick up the empty dishes.

I feel a hand land on my arm. "I got it. You cooked. I'll clean," Cooper says.

"Ari, if you'd like to go ahead and shower first that's fine," I say as she drops her napkin in the trash. "Maybe we can watch a movie after?"

"Ok." She smiles. "I really like the bath bombs Ivy picked out."

"Bomb away." I grin.

When I hear the click of the bathroom door, I let a sigh escape my lips. I could lie and say that phone call didn't rattle me a little, but it did. All his calls did.

Cooper is already at the sink, sleeves rolled up on his forearms, as he dunks the dishes under the spray. I watch the way they flex, my eyes trailing from the unintended sexy motion up to his profile.

It's not fair how gorgeous he is.

"Like what you see, Kota?"

I blink, quickly masking my blush with a swat to his arm. "I was lost in thought, not ogling you."

Geez, I'm lying left and right these days.

"You know, I'm your husband now. You can ogle me all you want." He wags his brows.

"You are my husband, aren't you?" I smile, leaning back against the cabinet.

He meets my eyes, his hands stilling on the dishes. He drops the plate, then flicks the faucet off.

"Don't move," he rasps.

I study him while he dries his hands, then fishes his phone from his pocket. He holds up a finger, signaling for me to be patient.

After a few taps, familiar music filters through the kitchen. He places the phone on the counter before offering me his open hand. "I believe I owe you our first dance."

I can feel the emotion rise in my throat as I place my hand in his. The song that plays has me holding back tears when he wraps an arm around my waist, tugging me to his chest.

Keith Whitley's *When You Say Nothing at All* plays through the speaker, taking me back to the very first song we ever danced to at the winter formal our freshman year. I was terrible, but he spent the whole night teaching me how to two-step.

He keeps one hand on my lower back, the other holding my hand as his thumb caresses my skin. My head rests on his chest, while the harsh reality washes over me. Some other woman will get to dance in his kitchen. Some other woman will get to be the reason for that bright smile. Some other woman will get to receive everything that Cooper Mayson has to offer, and that reality nearly buckles my knees. I'll have to stand by and watch. Smile, give my blessing, and watch him grow a beautiful family. *Without me.* But I'll still smile. I'll still be in the background, loving him from afar. I'll remember this moment. I'll remember the brief moment in time, dancing in this kitchen, what it felt like to be *his.*

Chapter Twenty-One

Dakota

"So, this is my baby." I slide open the latch to Rebel's stall.

He snorts, swishing his tail as I step inside.

This was the first horse I ever purchased on my own. I purchased him from Emmett, but I made him promise not to skim on the price. I wanted to pay top dollar. What he would sell him for to anyone on the market. The Mayson's had done so much for me, and even though Emmett tried to gift me the black beauty now prancing around his stall, I refused.

"Baby." Arizona peeks her head between the rails. "He's huge."

I chuckle, running my hand over his nose, before I lean in to kiss his neck. "Don't let his size fool you. He's a sweetheart."

My back muscles twitch as I maneuver myself next to him. We introduced Arizona to *The Sandlot* last night, and fortunately I fell asleep on the couch instead of in Cooper's bed. Which was probably for the best because after the day I'd had I would have most likely cried or climbed on top of him and let him hold me.

I glance back at her. "Want to give him some love?"

She steps back. "Hard pass."

"He won't hurt you."

"Not really my thing." She crosses her arms. "How did this become *your* thing?"

I run my hand along Rebel's back. "I've been around horses since I was little. Billy had a gambling problem and was always at the track. I think I became intrigued then. The speed. The power behind their bodies. The way they took care of their riders." I keep my hand placed on his hip, moving slowly around his back end before traveling up his other side. "Never ridden one until I came here for the first time for Cooper's twelfth birthday party."

"And you just hopped on?" She asks.

"Pretty much."

I remember than instant feeling of peace when I came to the barn.

"Horses have this emotional..." I pause, trying to figure out the best way to put it. "Intellect. They read body language. They read behavior."

"You're telling me that thing is an emotional genius?" She lifts a brow.

My laughter echoes through the stall. "In a way, yes."

Horses became my therapy. It was the only time I wasn't thinking about home. About when I would eat next. If we had electricity when I got back. I could just be a girl on a horse. *And it was magical.*

I'm lucky enough to have a full time job here at the ranch, that not only allows me to help train the colts, but I still have time to manage my personal sessions outside of the Mayson Ranch.

"I'll believe it when I see it," she mumbles.

Pressing a quick kiss to Rebel's jaw, I slide out of the stall and lock the latch. "Alright, let's go check on the boys."

"The boys?" She questions, falling in step beside me.

"I've been training three colts the last few months. They're being picked up by their new owners tomorrow morning," I tell her as we exit the barn and head toward the arena. "It's kind of bittersweet," I admit. "I'm proud of their growth but through the hard work, I tend to get attached."

A brief wave of panic hits me as we walk down to the pens. Will that happen with Arizona? I get attached just for her to be sent to a new home? A better place?

I spot Cooper first. He's leaned against the fence, his head tilted back in laughter as Clyde and Maddox join in.

A smile pulls at my lips as we approach. "Morning."

"Well, who do we have here?" Clyde tips his hat. "Looks like a mini Dakota if I ever saw one."

I smile and nudge her arm. "Clyde, this is Arizona. My sister."

He grins. "Nice to meet you young lady. You can call me Clyde."

"Clyde." She lets a smile form as she peers up at the old man. "Nice to meet you."

"He's like a surrogate grandpa." I shoot Clyde a wink.

"I'm here to serve."

I feel Cooper's hand slide around my waist. "Morning, wife."

Tingles skate along my skin, but I school my reaction. "Husband. You taking care of my boys?"

"Always." He juts his chin toward the next pen. "Got em' saddled for you."

My eyes scan over the pen, a sense of pride filling my chest.

"You did good, Birdie." The simple praise is whispered in my ear.

Like he knew I needed it.

My eyes connect with his before he slaps a palm to my ass. "Now get out there and show Ari what a badass her sister is."

Chapter Twenty-Two

Cooper

I watch closely as Dakota's shoulders finally drop, the tension leaving her body as we leave the courthouse. After waiting on her mother's death certificate, Arizona's birth certificate to arrive, and the multiple stops we made after the colts were picked up to officially make her a Mayson, she's finally relaxed.

We just filed the paperwork to request temporary custody of Arizona. They informed us we would be contacted by someone to let us know the next step and I already filled Norman in on the status.

"You alright?" I ask, holding the door open for her.

"I could use a drink," she mutters, walking past me and down the cement steps.

"Come on." I slide my palm along her forearm before gripping her hand in mine. "Fresh air will do you good."

She glances at our hands then at my face. "What?" I shrug. "I can't hold my wife's hand?"

She smiles, shaking her head. "I've never seen you hold hands with a woman in public."

I bump her with my shoulder before leading her across the street. "Never had a woman that made me want to."

Her cheeks blush, but she waves me off, thinking I'm just being *Cooper*. But what I'm really being is honest. She's the only hand I've ever wanted to hold. To proudly display for this whole town to see.

A few more steps, and we enter the Mayson Jar. The lunch crowd has already hit, the tables full and the atmosphere light.

Fern, the hostess that I've known since diapers picks up two menus. "Well, if it isn't the newlyweds." She eyes Dakota before lifting a brow at me. "You aren't pregnant, are you?"

"Fern." Penelope, my aunt, and the owner and operator of this fine establishment hisses before yanking the menus from her hands.

"What?" She gasps. "It's a fair question."

"It's rude." Penelope tucks the menus under her arm. "Why don't you go take your smoke break."

Fern rolls her eyes, muttering to herself as she waddles to the front.

"I swear, the older she gets, the worse the filter." Penelope grins. "Follow me."

I tug Dakota behind me, knowing that every eye in this place is on us. This is our first outing since the rumor mill picked up the wedding details, and there are a mixture of smiles and skeptical gazes. But I don't pay attention to them. I let Dakota slide into a booth before I drop down right next to her.

"I have to say, when your mama called me, I wasn't surprised." She places the menus down before she drops her hand on her hips. "Actually, you won me twenty bucks."

"What do you mean?" Dakota laughs.

"Just a little side bet I've had going with Shorty." She winks. "What can I get y'all to drink?"

"I'll take a water," I answer.

"And you, sugar?" Penelope says to Kota.

"Can I get a Shirley Temple?"

"Absolutely." She lifts a hand to wave at whoever just entered. "Be right back."

Lunch was delicious as always, and we only had four different people come up to us with a congratulations and an *I knew it would happen one day.* Every time someone said it, I waited for Dakota's reaction. Wondering how many times it had to be said before she realized the truth.

When we step out into the sunshine, I hear my name called from inside the restaurant.

Tim Ellis, the county commissioner stands from his table.

"Give me just a sec." I motion to Tim.

"Go ahead." Dakota waves me off, and I turn to meet him just inside the waiting area.

"Cooper." He holds out a hand. "Congrats on the new wife."

I chuckle, shaking his hand with gratitude. "Appreciate it."

He nods his head toward the doors, indicating he wants to take this conversation outside. I follow, glancing around to see Kota walking in front of the hardware store on her phone.

"What's up?" I lean against the outside of the building.

"I just wanted to give you a heads up. You can pass the message along to your father. Emmett and I go way back, and from one cattle rancher to another, I feel on a personal level as his friend that I should let him know when something comes through my office."

My spine stiffens. "I'm not sure I like the sound of this."

He blows out a breath. "Nothing concrete. But the RRC has been poking around. Talking about a pipeline. No specifics have been detailed but judging from their conversation it's sounding like they're looking out toward the ranch."

"Fuck," I mumble, my hand coming up to swipe across my mouth. We just made it through a fire that nearly shut us down, now this?

"Like I said. I've got no orders. But it's being tossed around. I know what your land means to your family and we try to do our best to protect it."

"Of course." I push away from the building. "Thanks for telling me, Tim. I'll talk with dad. Make sure he's prepared."

He dips his chin. "Gotta get back to the office. Tell Ruthie hello for me."

"Will do."

I watch him walk away, a heavy feeling weighing on my shoulders. Maybe it's nothing. Maybe it's not. But not even the heavy weight of that possibility fills me with unease like the sight across the street, and the man who currently has my wife pinned against the pharmacy building.

Chapter Twenty-Three

Dakota

My boots carry me up the sidewalk of downtown Mayson Ridge while Cooper talks with whoever needed his attention.

My phone vibrates in my pocket, so I slip it out before swiping the screen. "Hello."

"Hey, I just passed you. I would have stopped, but I'm heading to pick up Trace. School called and said he has a fever." Laiken sighs.

Her voice sounds tired and strained. My heart goes out to one of my dearest friends. She's tough as nails, but sometimes I wish I could swoop in and make everything easier for her. Turns out, I'm not the kind that makes things *easier.* I tend to make things messier. The first time I babysat Trace is convincing evidence of that. I was covered in baby poop from tank top to toes and managed to mix up the toothpaste and the diaper rash cream.

"I'm sorry, Laik. Do you need anything? I can pick up some Tylenol or Gatorade? I know he loves those animal crackers when he's feeling yucky."

"That would actually be wonderful. Mom is sleeping since she goes in at six."

Laiken's mom, Millie, works nights at the Silver Ridge Nursing home and is right up there with Ruthie Mayson on the list of the world's best moms. When her husband was tragically killed in a car accident, she continued to raise Maddox, Laiken, and Brady the best she could. Throw in Laiken's unexpected pregnancy with a low life who wouldn't step up, and Maddox's need to be Mr. Save Everyone, along with Brady's drunken outbursts, it was a tough time for the entire family. But Trace was the best thing to ever happen to our little corner of the world, and Brady may have had his fair share of trouble, but he was turning his life around. He'd become a firefighter and he and Maddox had been mending their strained relationship. Laiken had a harder time seeing the silver lining some days. And I don't blame her.

"Don't worry. Auntie Kota is to the rescue. Do you need anything?" I ask, crossing the street to The Medicine Box. The small pharmacy/grocery store on the corner.

"I'm good. You're a life saver," she says.

"Coop and I will drop it off. Take care of our boy," I say before hanging up the device.

My hand is resting on the handle of the pharmacy door when I hear the barbaric voice of none other than Joseph Terrell.

"Stopping by to get your herpes meds?" He sneers.

I freeze, whipping around to see the so called cowboy storm up the sidewalk.

"Fuck off, Joey," I quip, rolling my eyes.

Joseph works for Rocky Bernard. A ruthless crook with more money than he knows what to do with. Joseph trained horses on his ranch and was known for being cruel and unkind to the animals under his training. Which is why at least half of his clients are now mine.

"You think you're something special?" He growls.

I turn to face him, my chin high. If he thinks he can intimidate me, he's in for a rude awakening. I've been backhanded by my six foot four drunk father on multiple occasions. I can handle an idiot like him any day of the week.

"If you're mad about losing clients, that's your own fault," I say casually. "Maybe you should try actually taking care of those horses. Not abusing them."

His face curls into a snarl, his brown beady eyes glaring as he crowds into my space. "You think just because that Mayson boy lets you ride his dick that you're better than me? I know where you came from, girl. Know exactly what a whore like you does to climb the lad...."

"Joseph."

The simple name is said with so much fury that my eyes widen when I spot Cooper standing behind him. Along with Ryder. And Emmett. *Where did they come from?*

Joseph pauses, his head turning slightly to glare at the three men.

"Do you know who you're talking to?" Cooper asks, his hand flexing by his hip.

I've seen this move dozens of times. It means he's about three seconds away from causing a scene.

Joseph scoffs. "A no good *Sterling* is who I'm talking to."

I can feel myself flinch, but I still hold my head up, noticing the bystanders starting to focus on our little altercation. I'm sure a cell phone somewhere in the vicinity is capturing every horrifying moment of this.

"Wrong." Cooper takes a step, then another, until he's right in Joseph's face. "You're talking to a *Mayson.* My *wife* specifically." He peers down at Joseph, who all of a sudden looks scared shitless. "And let me make this extremely clear." Cooper pushes forward so his broad chest brushes Joseph's. "That is the last time you will speak to her, let alone look in her direction."

Ryder makes eye contact with me briefly before he idles up next to Cooper. Silence hangs, causing Cooper to lift a brow. "Do we understand one another?"

Ryder slips out his pocketknife, flipping open the blade before he starts to examine the shiny metal.

Joseph jerks his gaze from Ryder back to Cooper before he sputters, "understood."

"Good. Now get lost," Cooper grunts while Joseph scurries away, spewing profanities under his breath.

My eyes remain on Cooper, my stomach flipping at how he just stood up for me. How he's always stood up for me. *His wife.* I've never seen him that angry. This...*hot.*

With easy movements he reaches out, pulling me into his chest. One hand bands around my waist, while the other winds around the back of my neck. "You good?" He asks, his voice hoarse.

I nod, not being able to form words at how embarrassingly turned on I am.

"Good." He leans in, his voice a low warning. "I'm going to kiss you now." Then before I can blink, his lips crash to mine right there in front of God and everyone.

He sticks to the rules. Not even a touch of his tongue. But it doesn't matter. My toes curl as he pulls back slightly just to nip at my bottom lip before pressing a kiss there again.

When I open my eyes, he's grinning. My cheeks flame, and my knees go weak. Then I see the crowd formed, everyone still staring at us. The feeling of bliss immediately gets wiped away. Because for a split second, I had stupidly convinced myself that kiss wasn't just for show.

Chapter Twenty-Four

Cooper

The sun is barely above the ridges as I make my way to the barn with Dale on my heels. It's early, and even though the last thing I want to do is divulge in the news from Tim yesterday, I know I need to get Ryder in on it before it grows into something serious. Like us having to give up a chunk of the ranch against our will. I'd rather talk with him first before we break it to dad.

Ryder is already in the small tack room, a cup of coffee in his hand while Clyde shows him his new pistol.

"Morning." I wave a hand. "When Clint Eastwood is finished, I need a word, Ryder."

"Don't think I won't fire a bullet in your ass," Clyde grumbles, but I can hear the smile in his voice.

Ryder's heavy footsteps follow as I head to my office. It's not much, but it gets the job done.

"How's married life?" He asks, planting his ass on an old file cabinet.

I think back to yesterday when I selfishly took the opportunity to kiss her after Joseph nearly got himself smacked to the pavement. Did I use the situation to get my lips on her? Yes. I'm obsessed with the woman. Sue me.

"Well it's barely been seventy-two hours, but so far so good." I drop down in the leather chair, and face my brother.

His dark hair is shaggier than usual, but he has the same permanent scowl. He's not mad *at* me, but it seems like he's always mad at the *world*. He rarely spends time with us unless it's for work, and he seems to be most comfortable holed up in his cabin. *Alone*. We couldn't be more opposite, but he's the most honest, hardworking man I know. And if I needed him at three in the morning, you bet your ass he'd be there.

"And the kid?" He lifts a brow.

"The *kid* has a name. Arizona. And she's settling." I tip my hat up, running a hand over my hair.

"What's got you riled? Other than the woman you've followed around like a sad puppy since you were twelve thinks you married her for show?" He crosses his arms, a smirk forming beneath his beard.

"Sad puppy?" I scoff. "We all know I'm more of a golden retriever."

He snorts. "More like a poodle."

I flip him off before I turn my expression serious. "I ran into Tim at the Mayson Jar."

"And?" He presses.

"Said he heard a rumor from the RRC that they might possibly be looking near the ranch for land."

"Fuck...," he curses. "Possibly?"

I shrug. "He said it's just talk right now, but he wanted us to have a heads up. In case they come looking."

"Dad's going to flip." He sighs. "He's finally calmed down after the fire."

"I know." I dip my chin. "We can always fight it."

His phone pings inside his pocket and he slides it out with annoyance.

"Everything ok?"

"Yeah, it's just Doc," he says, thumbing a quick reply. "Got a heifer I need him to look at."

The fact he still has frequent contact with our vet, Perry Palmer always makes me want to ask questions. I'm sure he brings about memories Ryder would like to forget, but we've all been very aware *that* topic is off limits.

"She bred?" I ask.

"Yeah." He pushes to his feet. "About yesterday. That fucker Joseph bothers Dakota again, you say the word. I'll handle it."

There's that brotherly love.

"Thanks, man." I nod.

After he leaves, I do my rounds and meet up with the guys on the plans for today. The stalls need cleaning, and the fences checked for when we move the herd at the first of next week. It's almost nine by the time I line everything out and head back to the house to check on my girls. *My girls.* It's weird they already feel like mine. Mine to protect. To take care of.

I'm smiling like a goon at the thought when I open the door to the cabin, but that smile is replaced with compete shock at the sight before me. The living room looks like a supply closet exploded. Bottles of Lysol wipes are tossed throughout the room, accompanied by multiple bottles of Windex. The sink is full of dishes, the curtains off the windows, and all the bath towels are piled in the kitchen floor. My gaze scans over the mess, my eyes catching on Ari who stands at the dining room window, a rag in one hand as she mindlessly circles it in one spot with wide eyes.

I frown. "What the heck is going on here?"

Arizona moves her eyes to the other side of the room. "Ask her."

A curse sounds from the hallway before Dakota comes barreling around the corner, cloaked in yellow rubber gloves, and one of my white t-shirts. A red bandana covers her dark hair, keeping it from her makeup free face. Her blue eyes frantically meet mine.

"Kota." I point to the state of the living room. "Explain."

"The social worker called." She shifts on her bare feet, her purple toenails bright against the dark flooring. "They're coming tomorrow morning."

"Ok...." I draw out.

"I'm cleaning." She swipes her forehead with the sleeve of my shirt.

My hand brushes along the back of my neck. "Baby, this is chaos, not cleaning."

She huffs, her cheeks blushing because I just realized I called her *baby*. Like it was the most natural thing in the world.

"I just...panicked!" Her arms wave in the air. "It needs to be spotless. Perfect!"

"Ok, everything's fine." I start toward her.

"Everything is not fine, Cooper!" She shrills. "We didn't even have time to get the minivan."

"I'd rather take my chances with the sketchiest uber in this state than ride in a minivan," Arizona says as she tosses her rag on the counter. "And I agree with Papa C. This is chaos."

"Papa C?" I question.

She grins. "Has a nice ring to it, doesn't it?"

"Y'all are not helping." Dakota stomps her foot. "Hellooooo. We need the forces."

Moving quick, I bend, scooping her up and over my shoulder.

She screams, her gloved hands pounding on my ass as Ari busts out laughing.

"Hold down the fort, Ari," I call over my shoulder before charging to my bedroom.

If there's one thing my girl can stir up out of nothing, it's chaos. And hers has always been my favorite kind.

Chapter Twenty-Five

Dakota

"Cooper Ryon Mayson. Put me down," I command, my voice as stern as I can muster.

Except it's not stern. It's breathy and confused because my *fake* husband just nonchalantly called me *baby* then just proceeded to spank my ass after he slammed our bedroom door shut.

"Oh, full naming me now." He stops to ease me down. "I'm in trouble."

"Big trouble," I mumble when he stands to his full height just to peer down at me.

"I'm going to need you to reel in the panic for me, yeah?" He twirls his thick fingers in the air above my head and all I can think about is what those fingers would feel like...

I blink, shaking my head. *Nope. Not going there.*

"Ok." I take a deep breath. "I'm calm."

He snorts. "Right." He reaches out, removing the rubber gloves from my hands. "How about this. You take Arizona into town and do some school shopping. If she's going to be starting this week, she needs some supplies. A backpack. Those glitter pens or whatever the hell you used to draw on all of my notebooks in middle school."

"Gel pens," I correct as he places the gloves on the dresser.

"I'm sure she could use some more clothes too. A good pair of tennis shoes. Pair of boots."

"I think we might need to ease her into the boots." I drop down on the edge of the bed. "She's terrified of the horses."

Cooper sits down beside me, his legs spread wide. His thigh presses against mine, and my stomach flips. I've managed to keep this under control the last few years. I've gotten good at avoiding the *Cooper Effect*. But since the day he said those vows. The day he *kissed* me like I was really his, I've been struggling.

"Hey," he says, his palm settling on my knee. "You're not in this alone. I'm right here. So is a whole truck load of people who support you."

I close my eyes. "I know that."

"Then why the spiral?" He asks.

"There is no spiral," I scoff.

"Kota. You're wearing my clothes," he whispers, his hand squeezing my knee.

I clamp my mouth shut. Growing up, whenever I'd have a bad day, or a night when my dad was drunk and disorderly, I would always slip into one of Cooper's hoodies or shirts that I'd stolen from his room when he wasn't looking. I had stolen a bottle of his cologne too. Call me a criminal, but it made me feel safe. *He* made me feel safe in a household where love and security were nonexistent. I'm pretty sure he knew, but he never called me out on it. So anytime I'm stressed or just need to feel him when I know he can't be there to ease the pain, I revert back to fourteen year old Dakota. The one that desperately wished she was a part of a family like his.

"Yeah," is all I say, letting the silence hang.

"You know..." his voice lowers. "Have I ever told you that you look beautiful in my clothes?"

My breath hitches. My lungs burning as our eyes lock.

The look he's giving me right now tells me that what he just said...he means it.

The air thickens, his eyes dipping to my mouth. *Is he going to kiss me?* The hand on my leg slides up my exposed thigh, and right when I'm about to say *screw the list of rules,* a knock sounds at the door.

I clear my throat, jumping a few inches away from Cooper.

"Yes?" I call out.

"Um, some rando is at the door." Ari's muffled voice flows from the other side.

I'm on my feet in an instant, a wave of warning hitting my chest. *It's him.* The protective side of me flares, the need to shield Arizona from that monster is overwhelmingly strong as I rip the door open.

"What? Who is it?" I ask, peeking my head into the hall.

She shrugs. "Never seen him. But he kind of looks like Cooper, except he's like really grumpy."

I glance back at Cooper who pushes up from the bed. He grins, knowing exactly who it is and the wild rhythm of my heart starts to slow.

"I'll grab it," Cooper says as he squeezes past us.

I roll my shoulders back with relief as Ari gives me a confused look. "Well, who is it?"

I wrap my arm around her shoulder, guiding her back down the hallway. "You ever met a real life bull rider?"

She gives me a pointed look. "What do you think?"

I snicker before we enter the living room just in time for the stranger to saunter into the cabin.

"Well, look what the cat drug in," I tease when a cowboy walks in looking like he just pulled an all nighter.

Which he probably had.

"Arizona, this is Cooper's cousin. Meet the infamous Parker Stillwater."

Chapter Twenty-Six

Dakota

Arizona and I climb in my old Ford truck, waving at Cooper and Parker who are sitting in the rocking chairs on the front porch like two old timers in a John Wayne western film.

"So, I'm thinking if we hit the Smart Mart we can get everything in one swoop."

"What's the Smart Mart?" She asks, clipping her seat belt.

I glance down at her outfit. She's wearing jeans that are two sizes too big and a Justin Bieber t-shirt. She looks like she waltzed right out of the nineties if you include the elastic purple necklace around her throat.

"It's basically the knock off Wal-Mart. But it's got everything from groceries to clothes, so it's a one stop shop."

"Ok." She shrugs. "Don't feel like you need to butter me up with stuff. I want to be here, and I will tell that social lady that to her face."

I laugh, pulling out of the automatic gates. "I bet you will."

Silence engulfs us, but instead of embracing it, I crank the radio to some Tanya Tucker, roll down the windows, and try to make back roading on a warm Tuesday morning be a balm to both of our souls.

"Are you sure?" I ask, holding up the pink and purple sweater.

"It looks like a Care Bear threw up." Arizona scrunches her nose in distain. "I'm not really a pink kind of girl," she adds.

Noted.

"Ok." I hang it back on the rack. "Let's move on to the supplies."

I push the cart forward, happy that she at least picked out four new pairs of pants, six new shirts, and two new pairs of shoes. You would have thought it was Christmas morning the way she'd been smiling. *Over basic necessities like clothing.*

Another reason I'm internally cursing Bea Sterling at the moment.

We round the corner to the school supplies aisle, and she immediately beelines it for the sketch pads.

I let her pilfer, while I grab a few basics like number two pencils, erasers, some glue, a small pair of scissors, and some spiral notebooks. Out of the corner of my eye, I see her trace the edge of a book before she walks back over to me.

"Grab it," I say before placing a pencil box in the basket.

A blue one. Not pink.

"It's ok." She waves a hand. "It's pricey."

I roll my eyes, then march over to the shelf and grab two.

Her jaw hangs open when I motion to the wall of pencils and rulers. "What do you like to sketch with?"

"I…"

I move closer, my hand landing on her shoulder. "Ari, if there's one thing I understand about being your age, it's having an outlet. The one that lets you get your emotions and feelings out in your own way. If this." I hold up the two sketch pads. "Is it, then I will make sure you always have one on hand."

Her eyes hold mine for a moment before she moves them to the wall of pencils. "Those look really nice."

Her voice is quiet. Almost reserved, which judging from the entire week and a half that I've known her, isn't her normal.

"Then let's try them." I snatch up the pencils then aim my cart toward the front.

We almost make it to the checkout when I hear my name.

"Hey, Dakota!"

I turn to see Dean Vickerson striding in our direction. I would consider Dean handsome. He's tall, fit, and has a neatly trimmed dark beard that matches his dark hair. We've had drinks, danced, and worked together on some great horses, but I've never accepted his advances or join in when he blatantly flirts. I don't go there with clients, and there's the whole situation of me being hopelessly in love with my best friend.

"Hey, Dean."

"Hadn't seen you in a few days. Figure you'd be at the Mayson Jar at some point. Let me spin you around the dance floor a time or two."

It's evident he hasn't heard the news.

"I've been a little busy lately." I place my hand on Arizona's shoulder, who is currently giving Dean the death stare.

"This is my sister, Arizona."

He holds out his hand. "Nice to meet you. I see beautiful women must run in the family."

I inwardly cringe as she shakes his hand.

"Oblivion must run in yours," she says, smiling.

He frowns, trying to make sense of her comment.

"Well, we better get going. I'll be at the arena later this week," I say, moving toward the checkout.

"Ok. See you then." He winks.

Ari rolls her eyes, and I ignore her glances as we pile the items onto the counter.

It doesn't take long to check out, and only a few shoppers give us pointed looks of disgust before we manage to get everything to the truck. When I load the last bag, I feel Ari's hand on my back.

"Dakota."

I shut the back door before spinning around. "Yeah?"

Without warning, she launches herself at me, her arms wrapping around my torso. The hug makes my eyes prick with tears, but I push them back, and wrap my arms around her frame, hugging my sister for the first time.

"Thank you," she whispers.

"You are always welcome," I whisper back.

A few seconds pass, then she pulls away, turning to climb in the front seat.

She pauses, before peering back at me. "Who was that man?"

I laugh. "He's a client."

"He wants to date you."

"Well, he's out of luck," I say. "I'm off the market."

"Thank God," she mumbles before she slips in the seat and closes the door.

I can barely manage to keep the smile off of my face as I round the back end of the truck.

When I grip the handle, a piece of paper tucked inside my windshield wiper catches my attention. It's probably the pizza coupons the local arcade uses to draw in people on buffet nights. I press my boot on the running board and reach over to pluck it from the windshield. Only when I unfold the flimsy white paper, it's not a coupon. It's four words that make my blood run cold.

You deserve what's coming.

Chapter Twenty-Seven

Cooper

"I'm gone a week and now you're married with a teenager?" Parker says as he rocks back and forth in the rocker next to me.

My laugh is instant, my shoulders shaking as I move my own chair in rhythm with his.

Parker and I have always been more like brothers than cousins. He's only a couple of years older than me, and even though his mom, my mother's older sister moved them close to the Texas coast when we were only toddlers, he's spent every summer here at the ranch until he made it pro in the bull riding world. We traveled all over this state the minute we could drive. Going to as many rodeos as we could. I enjoyed the ride. Enjoyed the rush. But my life was here. I always knew that. But Parker? He had talent and determination like no one I'd ever seen. Which is why when ranch life called my name, the professional bull riding dream called his.

And I'm damn proud of him and his accomplishments. Even if it does take him all over the country.

"What can I say?" I lift a shoulder. "I've always been a family man."

Parker laughs, his head shaking. "You've been a sucker is what you've been."

I scoff, but don't deny it. I know exactly what he means.

"Was this her idea or yours?" He asks.

When I still don't answer, he fills the silence. "You've always loved her, Coop." He stops rocking. "You sure this is a good idea?"

"It too late if it isn't," I respond. "She needs me. She doesn't want Arizona in the system. It was the least I could do."

Parker is the only person I've ever revealed my feelings to about Dakota. He knows the truth. He knows she's been it for me. For *years.*

"Just don't want shit going sideways," he says, looking off at the field across from us.

"Speaking of sideways." I glance over at him. "How's Tori?"

His shoulders tense before he shrugs. "Tori."

I still don't have a single clue as to why he's with her. It's clear as day he doesn't want to be.

"I don't know why you don't just end it, man." I pull a toothpick from my pocket. "She's toxic as fuck."

"That's an understatement," he mutters.

"So, what's the deal?" I press.

"No deal," he says flippantly.

I call bullshit. No man puts up with someone like her for shits and giggles. And I'm one hundred percent sure it's not for love.

I pause, gauging on whether I should ask or not. I settle on, *why the hell not*? "What about Laik..."

"Don't." He holds up a hand, his jaw flexing.

"Ok." I close my mouth. "Off limits. I get it."

He pushes to his feet. "Just wanted to come by and check in. I've got the finals in Vegas in a couple of weeks. Had some down time. I'll probably go visit mom. Head out tomorrow morning."

"Alright man."

I stand to my feet. "Be safe. Keep your head straight. You got this."

He nods, but the look in his eyes tell me he's tired. He's worn. And I wish he'd stop keeping the secrets I know are destroying him.

"Later." He waves.

I watch as he pulls away, and not long after, I see a familiar Ford coming up the drive. This is how it's supposed to be. My girl coming home every night. *To me.*

Chapter Twenty-Eight

Dakota

I'm nervous. For multiple reason. For one, the note from yesterday. The one I tucked into my back pocket, then hid in my underwear drawer as soon as we got home. It could have been from anyone. My father had managed to make our family a lot of enemies, and it's not the first time someone had been a little over the top. Seeing as I haven't been notified of my father's release, it can't be him. I wouldn't even put it past that asshole Joseph.

I walk away from the window, then fluff the pillows one more time because apparently *throw pillows* are a deal breaker in a custody decision.

I'm slowly losing it.

"What did those pillows ever do to you?"

Cooper comes into the living room, looking way too good for someone I'm supposed to not want to see naked.

When I glare at him, he chuckles before he places his hat on top of his damp hair.

"When is she coming?" He asks.

The crunch of gravel sounds outside and my eyes widen. "Now."

Cooper smooths his shirt down, before he strides over to me. "Relax, Mrs. Mayson." He presses a quick kiss to my temple. "We got this."

If I wasn't already completely and utterly in love with this man, I am now.

Arizona comes from the guest room, a sketch pad gripped in her hands. "Time for the show?"

"She's here." I motion to the door.

"Ready?" Cooper asks.

"Totes," She chirps.

"Totes?" Cooper mocks.

"Totally," she confirms before a knock sounds at the door.

I check my outfit one more time. I changed out of my typical cropped t- shirt and Wrangler jeans for something that says *I'm guardian material* and not *I can shotgun a beer in three seconds flat.*

Moving to the door, I open it with a smile as I come face to face with a woman in her late forties. Her brown hair is twisted up in a clip, and she's dressed in a pair of tan slacks with a ruby red blouse.

"Hi. I'm Christine. We spoke on the phone," she greets.

Relief hits me at the fact she's not from Mayson Ridge. *Thank goodness.*

"Of course." I step aside. "I'm Dakota." I wave her in. "Please come in."

"I'm Cooper Mayson, ma'am." Cooper removes his hat as he holds out a hand. "Dakota's husband."

My cheeks heat, the casual way the introduction rolls from his lips, making me wish he could drag me around town and say it all day long.

"Nice to meet you." Christine moves her eyes to Arizona. "And you must be Arizona. I'm Christine."

Arizona waves with a brief "hi" before she goes back to her sketch pad.

Christine brings her focus back to us. "You have a lovely home."

"Thank you." Cooper presses his palm to my lower back.

"Well, maybe you can show me around and we can talk about what your plans are for Arizona?"

"Ari. Let's go check the horses while Dakota and Christine do a tour," Cooper suggests.

"Sure." She hops down from the barstool.

Once they leave, Christine follows me through the house. "So, you are Arizona's sister, correct?"

"Yes. We have the same mother," I answer before we move through the kitchen.

"I'm sorry for your loss," she says as we come to the guest room.

"Thank you." I gesture to the room. "This is where Arizona is staying. This is her room."

Christine scans the area before she faces me. "As her only living relative, you have a great chance of getting full custody if that's the goal."

"It is." I wring my hands together. "I don't want to be too blunt, but my mother was not the most reliable parent, and I want to make sure Arizona is loved and cared for the way every child deserves."

She smiles, before glancing down at the clipboard in her hand. "Would she attend Mayson Ridge middle school?"

"Yes." I nod. "Her education is very important to us."

She nods, jotting something down. "As from what I've seen, I'm comfortable recommending granting temporary custody. This would mean Arizona would be temporarily placed in you and your husband's care by a judge, then there would be more extensive research done to be sure this is the safest and best option for her. Arizona's well being is top priority."

"I agree." I move back to the living area, letting her follow. "What exactly is the timeline for something like that?"

"It depends. As long as there are no hiccups it could be a few weeks. Or a few months."

"Ok."

"In my experience, next of kin is usually the best option." She tucks her clipboard under her arm. "I do want to ask about her emotional state. The death of a parent can be overwhelming to a child her age."

"She's doing ok. She hasn't broken down crying or had an emotional breakdown yet. She seems very mature for her age, which makes me believe she had to grow up a little quicker than she should have."

"You don't realize how often I see that. It's sad." Her eyes soften. "I can recommend a child therapist that is very effective and affordable." She pulls a card from her pocket. "Might be worth a call."

"Thank you." I take the card. "I'm actually wanting to try something. I work with the child advocacy center twice a month. They bring a group of kids out to the ranch for equine therapy. You would be surprised at what a horse can do for a child that a human never could."

"I think that's a great idea." She smiles.

My chest feels lighter as we make it to the door. "If you don't mind, I'd like a quick chat with Arizona before I leave."

I smile, my heart finally feeling the lightest it's felt in days. "Not at all."

Chapter Twenty-Nine

Cooper

"Nope." I walk into the living room and yank the blanket off of Dakota.

I've let the last few days slide. She's made some excuse to be in the kitchen until an ungodly hour, or she falls asleep on the couch while her and Ari watch a movie before I can make her crawl into my bed. Which was part of the rules if she's forgotten.

"What?" She groans.

"We discussed this, Kota." I cross my arms as I stand over her. "My bed."

"I really am fine right here." She waves a hand over the sofa. "You know I'm a bad sleeper."

I stare down at her, unimpressed.

"Oh my gosh. If you're just going to hover like a creeper, then fine." She huffs.

Grinning, I step back and wait. Her eyes roll as she pushes up from the couch, then marches down the hall.

I lean my head back after seeing those tight as fuck spandex and a crop top shaping to her gorgeous body. I discreetly reach down and adjust myself before I follow. Flipping the hall light off, I make one quick glance behind me before I step inside my room and shut the door. Dakota is already crawling across my bed, gathering pillows in her hands.

"I can make a barrier." She places one of the king size pillows in the middle of the bed.

I let her have the illusion there will be any sort of barrier between us while I slide my joggers down my legs, leaving me in just my boxer briefs.

Her hands are still moving, but her voice trails off when I turn to face her.

She swallows thickly, her eyes hovering on my chest, before they travel lower.

"Here. Let me get that for you." I take two strides to the bed, then lift my thumb to the corner of her lip. "You got some drool there."

She blinks, swatting my hand away with a comical scoff. "I am not drooling. I was in shock. You can't just take your pants off without warning."

"And why not?" I ask, grabbing the pillow she strategically placed, tossing it to the floor. "Shouldn't a husband be able to strip in front of his wife?"

Her jaw hangs open. "Oh, so you're a strip tease now?" She laughs. "Show me your moves, cowboy."

She shakes her head, a playful smile on her face as she settles onto her side of the bed.

Pulling the covers back, I place both palms on the mattress, getting level with her face so my eyes hold hers. "Careful what you ask for, Kota."

She visibly gulps as she watches me slip in beside her. When I pull the covers over my legs and flick off the lamp, I let the darkness soak in. The only sound is her heavy breathing, and a smile blooms on my face. Her walls are crumbling. And it's only a matter of time.

My alarm hasn't gone off. The sun is barely up. But my eyes blink open because something warm and perfect presses right up against my morning wood. I don't dare move yet, afraid if I do, Dakota will pull her soft body away from mine. Her ass is pressed into my front, while my right arm somehow got draped over her bare torso, with my thigh slid right up between her legs. She's still asleep, but she's always been a squirmer. I close my eyes as she wiggles again, and my cock twitches against my will.

I internally curse as the steel in my briefs practically throbs when she lets out a light moan.

She's going to kill me before I've even had breakfast.

With the skill of a ninja, I manage to slide out from behind her, and escape to the ensuite bathroom to shower and relieve this pressure before I do something drastic like push her before she's ready. She's close, I can see it in her eyes. It's there. The feelings she tries so desperately to suppress. One day she'll see, and until then, I'll be right here. Waiting.

Chapter Thirty

Dakota

A horn honks, and I momentarily forget I'm in the school pick up line. Which is why I flip the ugly SUV behind me the bird before I pull up to the appointed lanes.

Arizona officially started school last week and I'm excited to see how her day went. She seems to be liking it, and she even talks about another girl named Heather that she met in PE that has become her new best friend. It warms my heart, but my nerves still swarm because it could be weeks before the social worker makes her final placement recommendation. Add that stress onto the fact I've been sleeping in the same bed with my *fake husband* for almost two weeks now with *nothing* between us. In fact, I wake up every morning with his body wrapped around mine, his unmistakable hardness pressed against my back, and very inappropriate thoughts about my best friend taking up residence in my brain. Like what it would be like to climb on top of him and feel that...

My truck door opens, and I jolt.

"Hey, how was your day?" I beam.

Ari doesn't smile; she just slams the door before yanking on her seat belt.

"What's wrong?" I ask.

"Nothing," she mutters.

I see her gaze move out the window, to a girl with fire red hair. The girl eyes Arizona with a smirk.

"Did she do something to you?" I narrow my eyes.

"Who?"

"Pippy Longstocking out there." I pull forward, easing past the group of girls huddled at the edge of the sidewalk.

"No."

"Ari. I don't care much for a liar," I point out.

"It's not a big deal." She rolls her eyes. "She just said some stuff."

"What stuff?" My hands clench the steering wheel.

"It's not..."

"Ari, if you don't tell me what she said..."

"She just said that I was trailer trash and that someone like me would never be invited to her birthday party."

My foot slams on the break. "Excuse me?"

"Her mom told her I wasn't allowed. That with a sister like you, I couldn't be trusted."

Fire ignites in my veins as I whip to the shoulder of the parking lot and shift the truck into park.

"She said what to you?" I ask again.

"Dakota, it's fine. I ignored her." She shrugs. "Her mom is probably sus anyway."

Speaking of her mom. I spot Pippy walking along the sidewalk with a woman I've had the displeasure of knowing since grade school. She was a bully then, and apparently, she still holds the title. And it's clear she's teaching her daughter to follow in her footsteps.

"Stay here," I murmur before my hand is gripping the latch, and I'm hopping out of the truck.

How dare she say those things. How dare she hurt my family. How dare she make her feel like less.

"Hey Molly!" I chirp, striding up to the woman who freezes a few feet in front of me.

"Dakota." Her smile is fake, just like her boobs.

"Can I have a quick word?" I ask, crossing my arms.

She gestures to the sleek Mercedes that's parked in the *no parking zone*. Figures. "Lilith, please wait in the car."

Once the little she devil is seated in her luxury seat, I change my tone. "Listen. I don't appreciate your daughter saying nasty things to Arizona. She's gone through a lot of changes in the last month, and it would be nice for her to be welcomed with kindness. Not judgment."

Molly practically gasps. "Lilith would never be tacky."

"Well little Lilith threw you under the bus too." I lift my fingers for air quotes. "*With a sister like me she can't be trusted.*" I drop my hands. "Classy."

"Well," she stutters before she yanks on her Coach purse. "It's true," she sneers. "People like you just want to latch onto people like us."

"People like me?" I take a step toward her. "Care to elaborate?"

She glances to her left, clearly uncomfortable by my closeness. "Don't cause a seen, Dakota."

"A scene?" I bark out a laugh. "This is a simple conversation, Molly. But know this. If I have to see that look on Arizona's face one more time because of the garbage you feed your daughter that bleeds over into her behavior at school, a scene will most definitely be caused."

A manic laugh escapes her. "Are you threatening the mayor's wife?"

"Threatening?" I laugh. "Of course not. I don't make threats, I make promises."

Her eyes widen as she shuffles past me, but at the last second, she puts the final nail in her overpriced coffin.

"Can't believe there's two of you in this town now. Guess I need to let my husband know it's time to clean up the trash."

You want to play dirty?

Game on.

Chapter Thirty-One

Dakota

"You can't be serious." Arizona practically bounces in the front seat of my truck.

It's almost midnight, and we're both dressed in all black. Down to the socks I picked up at the Smart Mart this afternoon.

"Deadly," I deadpan as I pull the black beanie over my hair. "You don't mess with my sister and get away with it."

Arizona smiles, her hands wiggling their way into a pair of black gloves.

Cooper is in the bunkhouse tonight playing poker with Clyde and the guys, which gave us the perfect opportunity to execute plan *Red Devils.*

"Now explain to me again the purpose of those." She nods her head to my back seat that currently holds approximately fourteen bags of fruit loops.

"I can't believe you've never heard of *fruit looping.*" I grab my tote sack and start to stuff the bags inside.

"Revenge is served a different way in my generation." She laughs.

"Well." I point up the road. "That house on the end of the street belongs to miss Lilith and Molly Whitehouse. The one with the perfect yard and overcompensated shrubbery."

"Isn't her dad the mayor?" Ari asks.

"Yes, but that's not important." I kill the ignition. "I have accurate inside information that tells me Molly is a bit of a yard nut. Has a special grass planted yearly, mows at least twice a week. You get my drift."

Arizona peers out the windshield. "So, what's the purpose of the cereal?"

"Look at it as a colorful dye job. Once these tiny circles are spread through the grass, then the morning dew sets in, its soggy city. The rain chance is just a cherry on top."

"Uh, I hate soggy cereal." She wrinkles her nose.

"As one does," I continue. "Once the cereal gets soggy, and wet, the color from the dye will then bleed into the grass, creating a colorful display of St. Augustine."

"No way." Ari snorts. "That's fire."

"Dang right." I wiggle my brows. "Now, let's show those goody two shoes just how *trashy* we are."

Arizona is peacefully drawing at the dining table while I'm whipping up some lunch. It's the second Saturday of the month, which means the advocacy center brings the kids out to the ranch in the afternoon for horse therapy.

The screen door slams, signaling Cooper's arrival. I glance up to see him remove his hat, a serious expression on his handsome face.

"Girls. The living room. Now," he barks as he stalks to the sofa.

Ari and I exchange glances before I set aside the loaf of bread, and we weave our way to the couch.

Cooper's forearms press down on his knees. "Heard a rumor this morning."

I tense as Ari shoots me a side glance.

"About?" I ask.

"Lilith Whitehouse was bullying Arizona?" He questions.

"It wasn't a big deal," Ari says quickly.

"You heard correct. And I handled it," I assure him.

He nods, his eyes meeting Arizona's. "I'm sorry. And I want you to know you can always come to me if you need to talk."

Oh, my heart. His kindness knows no bounds.

"Thanks, Papa C." She smiles.

"Well, you hungry?" I push to stand, but he holds up a hand.

"I'm not finished. I heard another rumor. Someone tie-dyed the Whitehouse lawn last night. You know anything about that?"

"Nope." Ari quips. "Zero knowledge."

I glare at her before facing Cooper. "Not sure what you're talking about."

"Really?" He stands, then struts to the front door, before reaching outside for something on the porch. "Must be a coincidence that I found exactly fourteen empty bags of fruit loops shoved in the barn dumpster."

Arizona's hand flies to her mouth, trying to contain her laugh.

Damn it. I thought I hid those far enough down. A freaking empty deep freeze box was on top of them.

"So, correct me if I'm wrong. Either you two were the culprits, or someone has a very unhealthy addiction to fruit loops."

I straighten my shoulders. "They're tasty."

He lifts a brow. "You fruit looped the mayor's lawn, Kota?"

"They deserved it," I shot back.

He drops the trash bag full of evidence, before he calmly walks back to the sofa. He eases down with a dramatic sigh. "I have to say. I'm extremely disappointed in you two."

My lungs pinch, the feeling of him being disappointed in me making my breath hitch. I hate it. And now I've dragged Ari in the mix.

"And I only have one question for both of you." He levels us with a pitiful look of hurt.

"Why the hell didn't anyone invite me?"

Chapter Thirty-Two

Cooper

My arms are hanging over the fence, my eyes tracking my smiling *wife* as she leads a boy about six years old across the arena. My chest tightens watching the progress she's made. She was once the little girl in that saddle, searching for peace. Now she dedicates her training and time to make sure these kids get to experience it even if it's only a few hours a month.

"Bruh." I hear from beside me.

I peer down to see Arizona next to me. "What's the *Bruh* for?"

"Are we going to keep acting like you aren't totally tripping over her?" She snickers.

"Tripping?"

"You look like one of those cartoon dudes with the heart eyes." She makes a heart shape with her fingers that resembles a gang sign. "I seriously can't believe she doesn't know."

I simply look back at my girl, not denying Arizona's observation.

"What are you going to do about it?" She nudges my arm.

"What do you mean?"

"I mean what's the plan. You got rizz. This should be a piece of cake." She climbs up on the fence to be eye level with me.

I chuckle because in the few weeks that she's been here, I've made progress in learning the lingo of a preteen girl.

"How about this. We make a deal."

She eyes me. "I'm listening."

"You get on that horse. I'll tell Dakota how I feel."

She frowns. "That's not fair."

"Why not?"

"Because he's huge. And I'm..."

"Scared?" I answer.

"Yeah," she admits. "I don't like that feeling."

"Neither do I," I say, sliding my toothpick to the other side of my mouth.

"You're scared to tell her."

"I'm scared to screw it up." I blow out a breath.

"I know I've only been around a hot minute. But coming from a place of zero love, it's easy to spot it when I see it. She may be too stubborn to admit it. But she loves you. A whole lot."

"How do you know that?" I feel giddy, like a kid about to blow out his birthday candles.

It's ridiculous.

"I've walked by y'all's room, and sometimes I see her pick up your pillow. She must like how it smells because she puts it to her nose before she hugs it tight." She shrugs before jumping off the rails. "I mean, it's a little creepy in my opinion. But who am I to judge?"

"Ari!" The little voice behind me reveals one of the coolest cowboys I know.

Trace runs full speed, jumping into her arms.

It only took one evening at a family dinner for Trace to deem her his new bestie.

"Can I show you how I ride Tater Tot?" He beams up at her.

"Duh," she says before he's on the ground again, dragging her to where Maddox is sitting by the pony in question.

A warmth fills me as I watch them walk away, before my name is called. My dad comes down the hill, meeting me at the fence.

"Need a favor. Got three colts that need to be picked up next Friday. I'd go but I've got that appointment with the lung doctor and can't miss. Can you and Kota pick them up?"

"Where are they?"

He shoves his hands in the pockets of his wranglers. "Lubbock."

"That's a drive." I whistle.

"Yeah. Probably have to stop for the night. Maddox will be in San Antonio with Havoc, or I'd ask him."

"Shouldn't be a problem." A spark of something like hope fires up in my chest.

The two of us.

Alone.

Overnight.

Away from Mayson Ridge.

I've been a patient man, but I think it was time to tell my wife that I was done with the charade. It was time to tell my best friend that I was in love with her.

Chapter Thirty-Three

Dakota

"How about we go down for a drink after I shower?" Cooper says before slipping off his boots.

"Sure." I nod, trying to think of any place to be besides in here while he's *naked* on the other side of the wall. "I need to call and check on Ari. I'll be on the balcony."

"You sure you don't need one?" He lifts a brow.

"Nope." I glance down. "I didn't get dirty. You did most of the work."

"Give me ten," he calls before he closes the bathroom door.

I slip outside, calling Ivy to check on Ari. Of course, she doesn't answer, so instead I take a seat on a plastic chair and gaze out over the rolling plains. It stretches for miles, and the raw beauty of it has my lips tilting up in a smile.

I was nervous to leave Arizona behind when Emmett asked us to make the haul to Lubbock, but Ruthie and Ivy promised me that she would have nothing but a night of snacks, pumpkin carving, candy, and a movie marathon. I reluctantly agreed and even let her invite Heather over to join the fun. Now I was sitting here questioning my life choices. Like the one where I surrendered to the wild idea that pretending to be married to the cowboy inside was completely rational. Just another day in the life of Dakota Sterling. *Chaos coordinator.*

We had driven a total of five hours today, stopping at a hotel not far from the ranch we will be driving out to in the morning. The ride consisted of my favorite playlist, my favorite snacks, and Cooper trying to convince me that Elvis Presley is still alive in some random mental institution. Needless to say, hours of being with the man in a contained space and not being able to climb across the console and kiss him stupid was doing funny things to my brain.

My gaze follows a group of fireflies when the sliding glass door breaks my trance. "Ready?"

Cooper grins, his damp hair peeking out from beneath his hat.

"Let's roll."

Following him out the door, we give a friendly wave to a couple walking past us in the hallway before we step into the elevator.

I settle against the back wall while Cooper presses the button for the first floor.

I lift my eyes just in time to catch his hand falling away. *His ringless hand.*

My stomach drops, my whole body tensing as I watch him slide both hands in his pockets.

He didn't wear his ring.

To a bar.

Out of town.

My fingers curl around the metal bar mounted to the wall behind me, my heart aching at the realization of what his intentions are tonight. I told him he could hook up with anyone out of town. I told him I would understand. Sure he refused, but that was weeks ago and he's probably folding. Probably having urges like any normal sexually actively male in his late twenties.

A sour pit forms in my stomach as the ding indicates we have reached our destination.

When the doors open, I dart forward, my eyes scanning the lobby.

"You ok?" His hand skims my lower back, guiding me to the left.

"Good," I croak, managing to somehow appear calm and collected. Not like I'm having a nervous breakdown over the fact my *fake* husband is trolling for a hookup at our hotel bar. *With me in tow.*

The bar isn't packed, but a few tables occupy guests, along with a couple of older men at the bar top.

As we take our seats, Cooper looks to the bartender who nods. "Tequila Sunset and a Miller Light."

A flicker of familiarity sparks in my chest; but I shove it away. He knows my drink because I've ordered it for years. Hell, Maddox and Ryder even know it's my favorite.

"So, how's Ari?" He asks, leaning back on his bar stool.

"Ivy didn't answer, but I left her a message to call me back." I tap my fingernails on the wood grain, scanning the female selection in the room.

A couple of ladies seem to be mid-sixties, not paying anyone any mind.

Another table is a group of younger women, and it's evident they've already spotted Cooper. Especially the brunette that's pointing and whispering to the girl on her left.

Maybe this is what I need. For him to sleep with someone. Squash this nonsense that I'm reading too much into. That this marriage could ever be *real.*

"Thanks, man," Cooper says before he slides my drink to me.

"Thanks." I pull the straw to my lips, sucking down the liquid that will hopefully chill my nerves and knock some sense into me.

"Excuse me. Can I get four shots of Crown?"

The voice comes from the brunette I clocked three minutes ago. She leans her elbows on the bar top, pushing up her cleavage as she turns to Cooper. "Hey, there."

He gives her a warm smile. "Evening ma'am."

She giggles. "Ma'am? You make me sound old."

I roll my eyes, sucking down more tequila.

"Just being respectful," Cooper says before taking a swig of his beer.

The brunette tilts her head. "You look familiar."

Cooper glances at me before he looks back to her. "I don't think we've met."

"Wait...you used to ride bulls, right?" She smiles, leaning into him. "I used to hang out with Pecos Holt."

"Holt? I haven't seen him in years." Cooper chuckles.

This is the thing about Cooper. He's mister sunshine. Never meets a stranger. And she happens to be a pretty stranger that would be straddling his lap if I wasn't moping on the stool next to him.

I mindlessly run my fingertip over the ring currently resting on my left hand. The one I haven't taken off since the day he put it on. I don't even want to psychoanalyze that right now.

"Yeah. Small world." She giggles again. "I don't remember you looking so handsome."

And that's my que.

I take one more gulp of my drink before I slide off the stool.

"Where you going?" Cooper turns to me and frowns.

"I'm kind of tired. Gonna crash. You two catch up."

"But..."

"Oh perfect!" She shrills. "Let me just grab my purse."

"Here." I fish the extra room key out of my pocket. "Take this."

"Why are you giving me the key?"

"Cooper. She likes you. She's pretty. Go have fun. I know you want to, and I already said you can have your pass when we go out of town."

His frown deepens, but before he can say anything else, I turn on my boots and bolt for the lobby.

A giggle sounds faintly behind me, and when I finally make it to the elevator, I let the first crack in my resolve splinter straight down the middle of my heart.

Chapter Thirty-Four

Dakota

It's been forty -five minutes. I took a quick shower, changed into my favorite t-shirt, then climbed under the covers so I could torture myself by watching the clock move slower than molasses. He was probably in her hotel room right now. Kissing her. Touching her.

"Stop it, Dakota," I scold myself out loud into the empty room.

It's about his happiness. Always. And if this makes him happy, then I want that for him. My hands come up to press into my eye sockets, the heavy feeling of tears forming behind them. *I will not cry.*

I will not prove to the universe that this is the most gut wrenching thing I've ever had to endure. Worse than him taking Shandi Turner to junior prom, where he got sloppy drunk, then proceeded to lose his virginity.

Taking a deep breath, I move to grab the remote when the beep indicates our door is opening.

I freeze, watching with caution as he walks in. His eyes remain on the floor, his hair tousled. Like someone's hands have been running through it. *I think I'm going to be sick.*

He walks into the room, dropping down on the end of the bed, never making eye contact with me.

This is too much.

I toss the comforter off of my body, my legs swinging to the side as I slide my feet into my slippers.

"I'm glad you're back. I'm just going to go get some air and try to call Ivy again," I rattle off before I swipe the key from the dresser. "Be back in a bit."

I go to walk past his silent form when a rough palm catches my thigh.

"Don't think so," he rumbles.

I pause, my breath catching as I stare at his hand.

"Excuse me?" I ask, my heart thrashing.

"You think we aren't going to talk about this?" He finally glances up at me.

"About you getting lucky with a buckle bunny? I'd rather not." I reach down and grab his wrist, removing it with a force I didn't intend. "I don't need details."

As soon as I take a step away, he pushes to his feet. "Why not? Best friends talk about everything right?" He grits out.

I shake my head, confused at why he sounds so mad. Ignoring his question, I head for the door, but I can feel him at my back. The heat from his body, the anger from his energy.

"I'd rather not talk about this." I reach for the handle, attempting to open the door.

"Why not, Dakota?" He presses before his palm stops the door from opening.

He never calls me Dakota. *Never.*

"What is your problem?" I hiss, shoving at his chest.

The door closes as he steps to me, pressing my back against the cold wood.

"Why are you so mad?" I ask, glaring at him.

"Why am *I* mad?" He asks, a sarcastic laugh rolling from his lips.

"Let's see. Maybe I'm pissed because you left me down there, practically on a silver platter to that vulture in heels."

"I thought that's what you wanted!" I shriek, irritated at this conversation.

"You wanted to go to the bar. You didn't wear your ring. I thought you were looking for..."

"For what? A quick fuck with a random woman while you, my *wife,* stayed up in *our* hotel room?"

I nibble on my lip. "I mean, I guess."

With a quick motion, his hand clasps the silver chain around his neck, bringing it up to dangle in front of my face. "This what you think I forgot about?"

There it sits. Right next to the cross pendent.

His ring.

"I didn't want to chance losing it out in that field when we had to catch those horses."

My eyes close when guilt washes over me.

He scrubs a hand down his face. "Do you have any idea how angry that makes me? That you think that little of me?"

I open my eyes. "Cooper that's not it. I just understand that you have needs and..."

He cuts me off, his hands coming up to grip my face. "Fuck, Kota. Are you tired?"

I furrow my brows. "What?"

"Are. You. Tired?" He says each word with frustration as I search his pained expression.

His thumb gently slides across my skin, tracing my jaw.

"It must be exhausting," his voice is almost a whisper, his lips moving slow and steady.

The bluest eyes I've seen to this day roam over my face, pausing to meet my gaze before he inches closer. His hard chest presses against mine, before he glides his thumb down the column of my throat. "Walking around every single day pretending you don't love me just as much as I love you."

Chapter Thirty-Five

Cooper

Dakota's eyes flare with surprise at my words. I sat down at that bar for over thirty minutes after sending the buckle bunny packing just minutes after Dakota left. I had zero interest in any other woman that wasn't the one currently in my arms. I sat and stewed. Going from shocked that she thought I'd actually take another woman up on her offer, to plain pissed at how we kept dancing around the obvious. The fact we were soulmates. Meant to be. Whatever other cliché phrase you want to label it. She knew it, and I knew. It was time to get past the walls she's built and own it.

"Coop," she whispers, her eyes filling with tears.

I press my forehead to hers. "I love you, Kota. You're my person. The first thing I think about when I wake up and the last thing I think of when I go to bed. I've loved you for over half of my life and we both know what this is."

Her sob is quiet but present. So I continue. "We both know this is real. You and me. It's always been real."

I pull away and tilt her head back. Tears stream down her perfect cheeks, so I trace them with my thumbs, silently begging for her to say the words. To not hide behind her fear. Her fortress of reasons she thinks she's not good enough for my love.

"Tell me." My voice cracks. "Please baby, tell me it's real."

She sucks in a breath before she grips my wrists, her walls finally crumbling brick by brick. I pull her close, letting her arms wrap around my neck.

"Please don't hold back," I whisper. "Let me love you, Birdie."

A sob wracks her body, her fingers curling into the hair at my nape.

Her voice is quiet, barely audible when she finally admits the truth. When she finally says the words that I'd been desperate to hear. "It's real."

My lips press against her hair, before she pulls back, looking up at me with so much emotion written across her pretty face. *Fear. Relief. Heat. Love.*

"Kota," I rasp, my fingers itching to touch her.

Every stubborn inch.

"I love you," she breathes out as she curls her other hand into my shirt.

Those three words are all I need. My mouth collides with hers, our lips moving with urgency as I scoop her up, allowing those long legs to snake around my waist.

Her back hits the door, while my hips pin hers, our bodies flush and hot.

She whimpers when I shift forward, the denim being the only barrier between my hard cock and her flimsy sleep shorts.

Her head rolls back, her neck arching so that I can slide my lips down the column of her throat.

"Coop." She gasps when I suck on the sensitive flesh near her collarbone.

My name on her lips feels different this time. It's a plea, a confession, and I can't wait a second longer to get this woman bare and discover every single thing that will make her say my name like that again.

I step back, bringing her along as she stays strapped to my chest. Her hips are frantically moving, her hands tightening in my hair as I stride across the carpet and to the bed. I lay her down gently, then stand up to my full height, just staring.

"What?" She whispers, her cheeks flushing.

"You have no idea how fucking perfect you are," I admit with a hoarse voice.

Her blush deepens, before she rises to her knees.

"I'm far from perfect, Cooper." Her hands cup my face, and I twist to kiss the inside of her wrist. "But if there's anyone in the world that makes me want to be it's you."

Her words hit me square in the chest, and I don't need any more confirmation. Dakota Sterling was made to be *mine.*

Chapter Thirty-Six

Dakota

Our lips meet again, and I swear a symphony plays somewhere among the clouds. His hands are everywhere. In my hair, on my waist, on my face. My tongue swipes out, seeking his as he pushes me back down to the bed.

He loves me.

Cooper Mayson loves me.

My body buzzes, my pulse racing as he kisses me like a man starved. Fire burns in my belly, an ache in my core so strong I can't help but grind my hips against the very protruding hardness pressed against my stomach.

"Cooper." I gasp, letting his lips trail down my neck. "I need you."

A growl sounds from his throat, before he bites gently at my lip.

Geez, that's hot.

His thumbs hook in the waistband of my pajama shorts, tugging them down my legs with a strategic slowness that has me squirming before they're even at my ankles.

"Baby." His voice rasps. "No panties?"

I grin, letting my legs fall open while I preen under the way he looks at me. Like I'm the most beautiful thing in the world.

His rough palm slides up my stomach, venturing under my t-shirt, inching between my breasts.

"I want this off," he says, before he gathers the fabric in his hands, then peels it over my head.

I lay completely bare to him. Spread out on a hotel bed while he towers over me, fully dressed. Something about it makes me feel needy. Completely at his mercy.

I can feel the way my nipples peak under his gaze, and when he drops to his knees at the end of the bed, then slides his callused hands up under my ass to guide me closer, I can't help the moan that escapes me.

"Does my wife need my tongue?" He asks, placing a hot kiss on the inside of my thigh.

Yes. Yes, she does.

"Yes." I pant, lifting my hips to urge him on.

I hear a light chuckle, then feel another kiss grazing along my opposite thigh.

My core tightens when I glance down to see him staring at me. *There.* His hooded eyes flicker to mine, before I feel his thumb slide lazily through my center.

"Are you always this wet for me, Kota?"

I suck in a breath when I feel the tips of his fingers tease me. "Have you been walking around all these years, just like this? Waiting for me to take care of you?"

Two fingers slide inside of me, and I arch my back.

"Yes. Yes, it's for you," I call out, my legs already falling slack.

"Shame. All you had to do was ask." His fingers disappear, but before I can protest the loss, I feel his hot, wet, tongue lick a trail up to my throbbing clit.

"Coop," I cry out.

"All you had to do was tell me you needed me." *Another lick.* "You know how many times I pictured this?" *Lick.* "How many times I've painted my shower thinking of my face buried between these thighs." *Lick.* "Your sweetness on my tongue." He lifts his head, locking eyes with me. "You full of *me*."

Who the hell is this man and what did he do with Cooper Mayson?

"I've waited a very long time to claim what's mine, Kota. And I'd like to do that right now."

I think I'm blacking out.

Letting my hands trail up over my breast, I watch his eyes when I pluck at the pointed buds.

"Then what are you waiting for, cowboy?" I widen my legs, letting them hit the mattress. "Make me yours."

With a wicked gleam in his eye, Cooper drops his head, his tongue doing things I'd never dreamed of, while my hands fist the sheets. His palm is splayed across my lower stomach, his other hand gripping my hips. I'm already seconds from falling mindlessly out of control. The way his mouth moves, the way his grip tightens. One more flick of his tongue and I crash. Burning up from the inside out. My cry echoes against the walls, my back arching as my thighs quake. My orgasm rocks through me, my body humming and pleased as his lazy strokes bring me down. My hips twitch when he glides over my sensitive flesh.

I sigh with content, just as a warm kiss is pressed against my center. Then I hear the familiar sound of a buckle and my eyes flash open.

"Don't look so surprised." Cooper stands at the foot of the bed, belt unbuckled, pearl snap wide open. "I'm not done with you yet."

Chapter Thirty-Seven

Cooper

I can still taste her on my lips as I tear my shirt off, then shove my jeans down my legs. I'm trying to be patient. To soak up every second of this because it's almost surreal. That she loves me too. That she's giving herself to me like this. I stand in my briefs, watching her eyes lower to the obvious bulge beneath the cotton material.

She wants this just as much as I do.

"Let me see you," she says the words quietly, her eyes finding mine.

Keeping her stare, I shuck off my briefs, my cock twitching at her sharp intake of breath.

Fuck, she looks so pretty like this. Cheeks flushed, lips swollen. *Nipples pink.*

With one stroke to ease the ache, I land a knee on the bed, before I'm hovering over the only woman to ever hold my heart. My eyes trace her face, before I drop a kiss to her forehead.

I've slept with women before. Most of the time those occasions spurred from too much alcohol and the reaction to her leaving with someone else. They never meant anything more than a way to deal with the fact that she wasn't mine. I know she isn't a virgin either, and although that thought makes me fucking feral, I know what this means for us. There's no going back. It's not a heat of the moment mistake. It's not fueled by alcohol and bad decisions. It's *real. It's raw.*

"I love you." The words leave my mouth as I hook her leg up over my hip, allowing my tip to press against her heat. I swear my eyes roll back from the contact alone. Her nails trial across my shoulders, her palm resting on my chest when she whispers back. "I love you, more."

With one surge forward, my bare cock disappears inside of her, pulling a gratified groan from my chest.

"Fuck," I grit out, holding my breath while giving her time to adjust.

She gasps, her eyes closing as she runs her hands over my hips. "Move."

With contained control, I retract my hips, before thrusting forward. Tingles shoot up my spine, my muscles clenching as she squeezes me like a vice. I've never felt anything this good. *This right.*

"Look how good you take me," I rasp, my eyes dropping to where we connect.

My hand slides behind her neck, angling her head so she can see. Her moan vibrates between us, the sound going straight to my dick that swells inside of her. I watch the way our hips collide, the slick sheen of sweat that's already coating our bodies as we move in unison. With a single move, I flip us over, then push up to my knees.

"Turn," I command, my hands maneuvering her so she's facing the mirror across the room.

Her back arches as she displays her perfect ass to me like a gift. With a palm gliding up her spine, I line myself up, then piston my hips, jolting her forward as she braces herself on the bed.

Her cry is like a match. Lighting me up as I sink in and out, my gaze locked on her face through the mirror.

"Open your eyes." My fingertips knead her hips, the hold almost harsh. "I want you to watch."

She moans, her mouth dropping open as her blue eyes lock with mine. My body burns as I pick up my pace, my pulse thudding as I hit deeper.

"Cooper." She groans. "I'm...."

"That's it, beautiful," I urge.

I can feel her walls contract and her eyes flutter closed. When she screams my name, I come on a groan, spilling myself inside of her as we keep our gazes locked.

It's the most electric thing I've ever experienced, and as she plants her face on the bed, her body full of satisfaction, I trail soft kisses up her spine, counting down the seconds until we can do it all again.

Chapter Thirty-Eight

Dakota

I have no idea what time it is. But I lie here awake, ghosting my fingertips over Cooper's chest.

"I'm sorry I never told you."

The hand resting on my hip squeezes.

"I never told you either."

I glance up, my eyes finally adjusting to the dark. We'd fallen asleep after round one, then I woke up, and wanted to know what he tasted like. *Insert round two.*

"I didn't want to lose our friendship," I admit. "I didn't want my reputation to taint yours."

"I don't give a fuck what anyone thinks." His tone is hard, and then all of a sudden, I'm being yanked up to straddle him.

"I think we both had our reasons. But I knew deep down you loved me. You just had those walls up." He tucks a piece of hair behind my ear. "I knew I'd break them down one day."

"Now you just sound cocky," I grin.

The sheets are bunched around my waist, my breasts exposed as he dances callused fingertips across my stomach.

"Not cocky. Confident," he corrects.

I tilt my head back on a laugh, then sober my expression. "I'm sorry loving me is so hard."

His brows furrow, then he scoots up to rest his back against the headboard. The movement makes me shift, causing me to rise to my knees, then settle back down.

"Loving you is the easiest thing I've ever done, Kota. I've been doing it since I was a kid."

My eyes well with tears, the reality landing on me that I've wasted so much time letting my circumstances block my happiness. Letting my family history derail the things I wanted for my life.

"I stole from you," I blurt.

A laugh barks from his chest as he leans over to flip on the lamp, then rests back against the headboard. "I know."

My mouth hangs open. "You know?"

"Of course I did."

"You know I stole bottles of your cologne?" I squint my eyes, watching for the lie.

He tilts his head. "Why do you think I bought two every time? I'd leave one out for you, and the other I kept in my closet."

"You never said anything." I swat at his chest.

He shrugs. "You weren't ready to hear what I had to say then."

"What do you mean?" I question.

He leans up, placing a kiss on the junction of my shoulder. "I mean, I wanted to tell you then that I was in love with you. That instead of you stealing my cologne, you could just come stay with me. Get out of that fucking house. Sleep with me every night so it would be permanently imbedded in your skin. That you'd always have me with you."

My eyes blink as he cranes his neck back to look up at me.

"We were sixteen," I whisper.

"I know." He kisses my jaw.

"But you slept with Shandi at prom," I accuse before embarrassment creeps up my neck.

I'm straddling this man naked and I'm bringing up a girl from almost ten years ago.

Just add it to the list of issues I have.

He shakes his head. "Not my finest moment. I wanted my first time to be with you." He takes my hand in his. "The only reason I even went to the lake with her is because you left with Carter Boyd. I heard him bragging about the plans you had."

My hands rest on his warm skin, a pain in my chest at the assumptions we both made. "I didn't hook up with Carter Boyd." I stifle a smile. "I actually kicked him in the balls when he tried to fondle me under my dress."

Cooper's head falls to my chest as he laughs, his shoulders shaking. "Then I walked home pissed that I broke the strap on my sandal. I had to save for weeks to buy those shoes. Then the next day, the rumor started about what happened with you and Shandi. I faked being sick the rest of the week so I didn't have to see you."

"I left soup outside on your porch for four days." He lifts a brow. "I even had mom make it from scratch."

"I'm sorry." I cover my face with my hands.

Our laughs fade away. The only sound between us is our steady breaths.

"I think we both did things we aren't proud of. We were kids, and you were dealing with stuff no one should have to, and I was just trying not to drown in the guilt that I couldn't fix it." His hand cups my jaw. "We both made mistakes. But I need you to know that it's *always* been you for me."

With my heart practically ready to burst, I press a kiss to his lips. "It's always been you too."

The gentle kiss turns deep, the emotion wrapping us in a blissful warmth. With a tug of the sheet, the barrier is gone, our bodies become one, and this time, I show my husband just how much I cherish *him.*

Chapter Thirty-Nine

Cooper

I should be utterly exhausted, given the fact we've both gotten a measly three house of sleep. We spent most of the night lost in each other. I think I told her I loved her a thousand times over the past eight hours, and she did the same. But I'm oddly refreshed. Dakota on the other hand, is pouting in the passenger seat, glaring at the woman in the drive through at McDonald's.

"And your egg McMuffin," she chirps at an unreasonable volume. *Even for me.*

"Thanks, Ellen." I hand her my card, then sit the bag on the console.

"First name basis now?" Dakota gives me a pointed look. "We've been at the window for less than three minutes."

"It's called being polite." I reach over and tug on a strand of her hair.

"It's called being an over sharer." She grabs the bag. "Was it necessary to explain why we are sitting at this window at six thirty on a Saturday morning?"

"She asked." I shrug.

"Alright, you two sugar dumplings," Ellen chimes when the window opens.

"For fucks sake," Dakota mutters.

"Here's your card, Mr. Cooper and here's that caramel coffee."

"Appreciate you, Ellen." I take my things. "Have a great day."

She waves before closing the window and I hold back my smile because I know Dakota is about to blow. If there's one thing she can't stand, it's loud, overly joyous people before eight o'clock.

"Your latte, ma'am," I offer.

When she goes to take it, I pull it back, stopping at the edge of the parking lot.

"Hey," she chides.

I lean across the console. "You want to thank me properly?"

"Cooper, as much as I love you, it's entirely too early for a blow job."

A laugh filters from my mouth, my head shaking at her scowl. "I meant a kiss, darlin. But I'd take a roadie anytime."

"You would." She rolls her eyes, but I see her small smile as she leans in to press a kiss to my lips.

Something I'll never get tired of.

"That's all I wanted." I hold out the coffee.

"Thank you," she whispers as she wraps her hand around the cup.

After taking a sip, she slides on her shades, preparing to leave me to drive while she falls asleep.

"Now." I pull out onto the highway. "What's your theory on Princess Diana?"

Dakota groans dramatically, her head dropping against the head rest in agony.

A smile spreads across my face because as much as she hates mornings, and probably me right now, I know she'll humor me the entire way home.

It's already dark by the time we make it back to the ranch. After unloading the horses and getting them settled, we drive the ATV over to Maddox and Ivy's cabin to pick up Arizona who hitched a ride after leaving my aunt Penelope's. Mom and dad were staying there until the farmhouse was finished. Which by the looks of it, it won't be much longer.

When we pull to a stop, I feel Dakota take my hand in hers to stop me from getting out.

"Hey." She tugs.

"Everything ok?" I wrap an around her shoulder.

“Everything is great.” She blushes. “I just.... this.” She points between us. “Happened. Finally.” She laughs. “And it’s wonderful. And perfect...”

I take her chin between my fingers. “And you’re not ready to tell.”

Her eyes soften. “I know how people will react. Don’t get me wrong, I know everyone we love will be on cloud nine. But I kind of just want to enjoy this without all the questions and fuss. We’ve only been in our little bubble for barely twenty-four hours. I’m not ready for it to pop.”

I lean in and place a kiss on her forehead. “If that’s what you want, I have no problem keeping you to myself.”

She laughs. “Especially with everything going on with Ari. Let’s just get through that, then we can let everyone know that I’m your girlfriend.”

“Wife,” I correct.

She waves a hand. “You know what I mean. We kind of went ass backwards.”

“But just so I can sleep at night.” I tuck a piece of hair behind her ear. “You want this?”

Her eyes search mine. “I’ve always wanted this.”

“Good.” I release her. “Let’s go get our girl.”

Chapter Forty

Dakota

Ari sits in the front seat next to me, an ice cream cone perched in her hand. It was Sunday, and that meant we were indulging in some *girl* time. After we checked in on the colts this morning, Cooper sent us away to enjoy a movie and ice cream while he helped Ryder get a plan for moving the herd. Apparently, they were starting the move tomorrow and it would take a few days to get all the cattle accounted for and sorted.

"I can't believe you don't like cookie dough," I gasp as we pull out onto the highway that leads to the ranch.

"And I can't believe you don't like pineapple."

"That's a fruit. Not a dessert." My finger twists the knob to turn up the radio.

I learned that Ari seems to favor Ty Myers. I was even secretly trying to find tickets to his next concert to surprise her with on her birthday. Which happened to be in two short weeks.

"It's just a little sus," she mutters before biting into her waffle cone.

I laugh, glancing in my rear view mirror at the truck coming up behind us. He seems to be in a hurry, and I'm expecting him to pass me even though I'm driving a steady seventy-five. When he approaches my bumper, following a little too close for comfort, I slowly move to the shoulder to let him pass.

He doesn't.

Squinting in the side mirror, I try to see the make and model. Looks like a black dodge. Older model. License plate looks custom. *BRR*. I tear my eyes from the mirror with a frown. Drifting back in my lane, my pulse picks up as Ari sings quietly next to me. I let my boot press harder on the gas, hoping to pull away from the asshole who clearly didn't know how to drive. Unfortunately, we get a lot of those in these parts. But he eats up the space, his front end so close that I can't even see the grill anymore.

Something is off.

As soon as the thought occurs, a jolt rams us forward, the force so sudden Ari's ice cream flies into the windshield.

"Shit," I curse, gripping the steering wheel.

"What was that?" Her grip tightens on the seat, her head swiveling to look behind us.

Another force comes, the crunching of metal roaring as he rams into my tailgate.

"Hold on, Ari!" I shout, trying to maneuver us from the shoulder.

Before I can right the wheel, the dodge speeds up, using his front fender to jar into my driver side door. The impact sends us barreling straight for the ditch.

"Dakota!" Ari shrieks, panic evident in her voice as my foot darts to the break.

I'm not quick enough to slow us down. My tires hit the loose gravel, spinning us in a half circle, before the guard rail connects with the back passenger side of my truck.

The hit causes my head to bounce off of the window, pain searing through my temple as my vision blurs. On instinct, my hand reaches for Ari, my eyes blinking as she sits frozen.

I can vaguely hear the dodge rev its engine in the distance when I finally gain my composure.

"Are you ok?" I croak, my hands checking over her body.

"I'm ok." Her voice shakes, before she faces me.

Her eyes widen, her hands trembling. "You're bleeding!"

"What?" I reach up to my temple, then bring my hand down to see my fingertips coated in blood. "I'm fine," I assure her.

I glance around the cab, trying to find my phone. I spot it in the floorboard beneath Ari's feet.

"Grab my phone."

She scrambles for the device, handing it over as I try to still my shaking hands. With my pulse still thumping and my heart pounding, I dial three numbers.

911.

Chapter Forty-One

Cooper

Ryder adjusts his hat before standing from the chair across from my desk. We had a game plan for tomorrow morning, and with all hands on deck, we figured three days was plenty to get the job done.

Maddox is seated on the edge of an old file cabinet, smiling at his phone like a lovesick fool. Not that I'm complaining. I'm stoked that he loves my sister so much.

"Y'all got plans?" I ask.

Ryder shrugs. "Maddox mentioned something about dove hunting in a couple of hours."

Maddox lifts his head. "Saw some in the pasture behind our cabin. Perfect spot."

"You coming?" Ryder asks.

"Yeah. Let me check with Kota."

Ryder just shakes his head before leaving the office while Maddox chuckles. "You got it as bad as I do."

Pushing to my feet, I shoot him a look. "Think so?"

He slaps a hand on my shoulder. "Coop, you ain't fooling nobody. Especially me."

My laugh echoes in the barn as we walk through the alleyway. My boots hit the gravel when my phone rings.

I frown, swiping the screen. "This is Cooper."

"Cooper, it's Jefferson."

I freeze at the sound of the familiar officer's voice. "What happened?"

"There's been an accident."

The sliding doors to the ER part as I storm through the opening. Maddox barley got the truck stopped before I was climbing out and hauling ass inside the building.

The first person I see is Jefferson. He's Ivy's age, but I knew him well.

"Where is she?" My throat feels tight and my skin taunt.

He holds up his palms. "She's ok. No one was seriously injured."

I stop right in front of him, peering down into his eyes. "Jefferson. I'm only gonna ask you one more time. Where is my *wife?*"

He swallows, taking a step back. "Follow me." He turns on his heels. "But you need to calm the fuck down, Coop. You'll scare them."

Them. Shit, Ari.

He leads me back to a room with a few curtains separating beds along the back wall. He motions to the one on the far right.

"She's right here."

It seems like it takes an eternity to cross the room. My hand grips the white curtain, and I slowly slide it back, revealing my entire world sitting cross legged on a hospital bed, talking to an officer. A bandage is placed over her temple, and her hair is piled up on top of her head.

Blue eyes meet mine and she immediately jumps from the bed. Relief sweeps through me the second her body is against mine.

She's ok. Alive.

"I'm here," I whisper into her hair.

She sniffs, her arms winding around my neck.

"Is Ari ok?" I ask, kissing her hair.

"She's ok. The nurse took her down to get a snack in the cafeteria."

She pulls back to look at me. "It could have been so much worse."

"What happened?" I ask, running my finger over the skin by her bandage.

"Mrs. Mayson. I hate to interrupt, but I need to finish getting your statement. It's usually best when the incident is fresh." The female officer gives a gentle smile.

Incident?

"You were in a car accident. Was someone else involved?"

Dakota steps away, climbing back onto the bed. I already hate the distance, so I follow, pulling up a chair next to the bed and grip her hand in mine.

"Let's start from the beginning." The officer clears her throat. "Start when you left the ice cream shop."

Dakota squeezes my hand, then begins to recite what happened.

Fire swims in my veins the more she reveals. The black dodge. The aggressive behavior. I was so fucking mad I almost missed her last words.

"Wait, what?" I scowl. "He rammed you off the fucking road?"

"Yes. He hit us three times," Dakota says, her hand tightening in mine.

Someone hit her on purpose.

"Is there anyone you can think of who would do this? Anyone that has possibly become an enemy?" The officer asks.

My eyes catch on Dakota's and for a split second, fear slashes across her face.

"I mean…not off the top of my head."

"Her father," I state.

"Your father?" She lifts a brow at Dakota.

"It can't be him. They are supposed to notify me if he gets released." Dakota frowns. "I haven't gotten anything."

"He's in prison?" The officer jots something on her notepad.

"Yes. He called me a few weeks ago and told me he was getting out, but I haven't heard from him since. We don't communicate often. He usually spits lies anyway." Dakota fidgets with a white blanket on the bed with her free hand. "The courts are supposed to send me a letter notifying me of his release."

"Ok. Has there been anything else? Anything suspicious?"

She goes to answer no but pauses.

"What is it?" I press.

"A note." She shakes her head. "I chalked it up to someone just being an ass."

“What note? You didn’t tell me about a note?” Suddenly, my anger is back in full force.

“I know. I wasn’t even sure what it was.”

“What did it say?” The officer asks.

“It said, *you deserve what’s coming.”* Dakota drops my hand and leans her head down. “I thought....”

“Someone is stalking you.” My tooth practically cracks as I clench my jaw. “You need to find Billy Sterling. Now.”

“Why would he want to hurt you?” The officer asks, glancing at her notepad.

Dakota hesitates before peering over at me, the memory of that day still heavy on her heart. “Because I’m the one who put him in prison.”

Chapter Forty-Two

Dakota

Eighteen

The lights from the racetrack fade into the background as we pull out onto the highway. My hands clench against my jeans as Billy presses on the gas, going way too fast for someone that's had almost an entire bottle of whiskey. He's pissed because he lost. Again. And since I didn't deliver him the knowledge of which horse was head of the ranks today, I'm on his shit list. Shocker. The only reason I even agreed to come is because he threatened to sabotage the Mayson Ranch. Apparently his newest "job" was working for Rocky Bernard, who happened to be a snake disguised as a wealthy hard working rancher. His ranch butts up to Cooper's family ranch, and Billy was descriptive on the ways he would make their life hell.

So here I sit, sweaty and furious that I still bow to his manipulative bullshit. But I know firsthand the cruelty of Billy Sterling. And I'd do anything to protect the Mayson's.

"You're just about as worthless as your mother was," he sneers as he swerves, barely missing the bumper of a Sequoia.

"Funny. Everyone around town thinks I get it from you," I toss out.

Wrong move.

I barely have time to react, before the back of his hand is slamming against the side of my face.

The force has my head bouncing off of the window, the searing pain shooting from my temple to my jaw.

"Keep running that mouth and your little boyfriend gets it," he growls.

I right myself as fury wraps around my throat. I curl up my fist, my jaw clenching. Before I can make a stupid decision, like clock this bastard and crash this truck, blue and red lights flash behind us.

Billy curses, then abruptly swerves to pull over to the shoulder past the Welcome to Mayson Ridge sign.

The cruiser slows behind us, coming to a stop as Billy's brow begins to sweat.

A tap at my window has me rolling it down, my eyes meeting the officer standing next to the truck.

"Evening." He tips his cowboy hat.

"There a reason you pulled me over?" Billy snaps.

The cop lifts a brow. "Got a call about reckless driving. License and insurance."

Billy grumbles under his breath before pulling out his ID. I hand it over to the cop, and he retreats to his car.

"I ain't done shit wrong," Billy says, his hands gripping the steering wheel in frustration.

Not three minutes later, another squad car joins, and two cops approach.

"Mr. Sterling. I'm going to need you to step out of the vehicle." The officer at my window motions. "Officer Fawn is waiting on the other side.

"What the fuck for? I didn't do anything," Billy shouts, his eyes wild.

"Can you step out ma'am?" The officer softens his voice.

I nod, sliding out of the truck, my boots landing on the asphalt. As I shut the door and face him, he stills when he sees my cheek. I'm sure it's red and swollen at this point.

"You his daughter?" He asks, his eyes full of empathy.

"Yes."

"Has he been drinking?" He asks.

I nod. "Yes."

"I'm officer Brandt. Come stand by my cruiser, please." He guides me to the back of the truck, over to where his car is idled.

The other officer is giving Billy a sobriety test, that he's clearly failing.

"I'm going to search the vehicle. He's under the influence," Officer Brandt calls before he slides on a pair of black rubber gloves.

I breathe through my nose, my chest pounding as I watch the scene unfold. Billy cursing Officer Fawn. Curious cars slowing as they pass. Embarrassment flooding my skin that the whole damn town is witnessing this debacle.

Then officer Brandt steps back from the truck, a black backpack in hand. I don't recall seeing it when I got in the truck before the races. When he unzips it, some of the contents spill out onto the ground.

Baggies.

"Fawn!" He shouts. "We need backup."

He digs into the bag, removing a small scale.

"Mr. Sterling." Officer Brant raises up, holding the white baggie in the air. "Is this your paraphernalia?"

"That shit ain't mine!" He scoffs.

"Well, there's plenty of eight balls ready to go in this bag." He drops them back into the backpack. "They just magically appear in your back floor board?"

"It ain't mine!" He roars. "You planted that shit!" Billy jerks, but Officer Fawn takes him to the ground, cuffing his hands behind his back.

"What's your name ma'am?" Office Brandt asks.

"Dakota." I swallow, not believing the scene in front of me. "What's in the bag?"

"Looks to be cocaine." He brings the backpack to his cruiser, speaking into the radio clipped to his shirt.

"Did he do that to your face?" He asks.

"Yeah." I touch my cheek.

"This a reoccurring event?"

"Unfortunately." I let my hand slide into my back pocket.

The urge to call Cooper is strong. Almost overwhelming. What if they think it was mine? That I helped him.

Panic takes root in my chest.

"I have to ask, is that bag yours?" He faces me.

"No. It's not mine." I shake my head.

Another cruiser pulls up, along with the sheriff. My gut churns, the thought that it could finally be the day my father drags me down with him.

"I just need confirmation." He reaches out to gently touch my shoulder. "I know he's assaulted you. I know he's been drinking, and I know he was driving reckless."

I blow out a breath before he continues.

"But I need to know if that's his backpack. Have you seen it anywhere else? At your house? His work?"

I nibble on my lip, my pulse skyrocketing as I watch them lower Billy into a police car. They're taking him away. Finally. But he always comes back.

I lock eyes with Officer Brandt and do what I should have done years ago. "It's his."

He dips his chin. "You have someone you can call?"

"Yes."

"Good. Let's get you settled back here until your ride comes. He won't be going home tonight or anytime soon."

As I slide into the back of the police car, I shakily pull out my phone before pressing the contact at the top of my list.

He answers on the second ring.

"I'm ten minutes from getting on a bull. If your ass is not in those stands in fiv.."

"Coop," I say quietly.

He goes silent.

A beat passes.

"Birdie."

"I need you."

There's no hesitation. "Text me the address. I'm on my way."

When he ends the call, I stare ahead, watching the blue and red lights flash.

I'm free.

He's gone.

But my freedom will only last so long. One day he's going to want revenge. Because the truth is.... I've never seen that bag in my entire life.

Chapter Forty-Three

Cooper

It took almost three hours for the police to get the information they needed and for the doctor to release Kota and Ari. Ari is currently drawing on a notepad that a nurse let her borrow. Thankfully she came out of the accident without a scratch. Dakota keeps glancing over at her, and I can already read the look in her eyes. She blames herself.

We're waiting on the nurse to bring the discharge papers when the curtain sweeps back and Christine steps inside. I can practically see the blood drain from Dakota's face.

"Christine." She slides off the bed.

"Hi. I got word you two were in an accident and I wanted to check in. I was actually planning a surprise visit this evening, but I figured it would be less hassle to just come here and check on Arizona."

"Of course." Dakota waves her in.

Ari looks up and gives a small smile. "Hey." She darts her gaze to me.

"Hey, Arizona. You ok?" She asks.

"I'm good. Not even a bruise." She motions her hand. "Dakota got the brunt of it."

Christine nods, her eyes focusing on Dakota. "Mind if I speak with Arizona in private for a moment?"

"Is that ok with you, Ari?" Dakota asks.

"Yeah. That's fine." She shrugs.

"Here." I pull out my wallet and take out a few dollar bills. "Why don't you grab you a snack from the vending machine down the hallway."

Ari pushes to her feet, taking the money before she follows Christine. As soon as they disappear down the hallway, Dakota sinks to the bed.

"She's going to take her away." Her voice cracks.

"Baby. Look at me." I walk over, crouching down in front of her. "No one is taking her away."

"They will," she hisses. "I almost got her killed today!"

I capture her hands in mine. "You did nothing wrong."

"But it's my fault," she argues. "Someone literally tried to kill us, Cooper. Me." She points at her chest. "Ari was just collateral damage. I brought that danger to her."

I intertwine our fingers. "What happened was twisted. And I promise you that I will not stop until I find the asshole who did this."

She nods, her eyes closing.

"But you need to hear me," I say, clearing my throat. "You are not responsible for someone else's actions."

"But if it's him. It's my fault," she whispers.

"No. If it's him, he's just proving why he should be locked up behind bars for the rest of his life."

I push to stand, dropping a kiss on her forehead. "I need you to stay with me, Kota. With Ari. Don't go rogue because you're convinced this is on you."

"We're back," Arizona announces as she takes her spot in the chair.

Christine smiles. "Do you two have a minute?"

I nod and hold my hand out to Dakota. She takes it, then we follow Christine over near the nurse's station.

"Arizona told me what happened, and I'm so sorry someone did that to y'all," she begins. "I'm glad no one was seriously hurt."

"Thank you." Dakota blows out a breath. "It was unexpected."

"I do have a question." She glances around. "It's my job to investigate thoroughly. And I'll be honest. I haven't come across anything to paint either of you in an ill light."

My hand rubs up Dakota's arm, tugging her into my side for comfort.

"But I am concerned about your father and his release." Her eyes meet Dakota's. "From what I gather he is dangerous. Would he be directly involved with Arizona? Are you planning on reconnecting with him?"

"Absolutely not," Dakota answers. "I broke ties with him years ago. He's called a handful of times since being in prison. We've had only a few conversations. He has no place in my life, and especially not in Ari's."

"Dakota has not been notified of his release. We are not sure he is even out yet," I add.

"Ok. I understand." She adjusts her purse. "I want you to know I'm sorry for the situation. I'm just doing my job. Arizona's safety is my priority."

"She's safe," I assure her. "The ranch is the safest place she can be."

"I will keep in touch and notify you when I plan to do my final home visit." Christine gives Dakota's arm a gentle squeeze. "Take care."

When she leaves the space, I can feel the tension coiling in Dakota's frame. "I'll never be rid of him. Will I?" She looks up at me. "He's not even here and he still manages to ruin any good thing I have."

Cupping her face, I smooth my thumbs over her cheeks. "Not this time, Birdie. He won't win this time."

Chapter Forty-Four

Dakota

This is what family is.

Ruthie is in the kitchen of our cabin, rolling dough as Trace giggles next to her. Arizona is even in on the baking. She's cutting out tiny ghosts and pumpkins, sitting them aside to be popped in the oven. Ivy and Laiken are sitting with me on the sofa, hot cups of coca filled with marshmallows as Cooper, Ryder, Maddox, and Emmett sit at the table, pretending they aren't plotting some covert revenge plan. *My family* is here, showing their support when we were shaken up.

"Mom came home all smiles today." Laiken smirks. "Guess who made an appearance at Silver Ridge."

"It can't be," Ivy grins, licking the foam from her top lip. "I figured after Ray passed that Preston wouldn't have any reason to come back."

"Mom said he's donating all the money for the new wing at the nursing home in honor of Ray."

A smile hits my lips. I remember Ray and his wife Cecile being one of the only residents that always showed me kindness as a child. Their kids too. Preston Rusk was basically a Mayson Ridge legend. The one and only to go all the way to the NFL. An injury spurred an early retirement, which led him to coach college football for a few years, then eventually, he found his way back to coaching one of the top teams in the NFL. I wasn't much of a football girl, but when someone makes it big from a town as small as ours, everyone becomes a part of the celebration.

"Anyway. I just thought it was really cool of him. His wife was with him too." Laiken wiggles her finger to wave at Trace. "It's refreshing to know there are still good people in this world."

I appreciate Laiken's words. Her intentions of showing me that kindness does exist after the day we had.

My skin tingles, the awareness that a pair of eyes are on me. I don't have to guess. Cooper has been watching me like a hawk all evening. Like my father himself was going to break down the door and steal me right off of this couch.

Our eyes meet over Ivy's shoulder, and per usual, my heart flutters. But this time it was different. I knew this man *loved* me. I knew what his light felt like and I couldn't believe it was actually mine to bask in.

"First batch is ready!" Ruthie grins, making a *tada* motion at the cute sugar cookies spread across the island.

"I even added sprinkles." Trace beams. "This one is for you, Kota."

I smile at the use of the nickname. Typically, Cooper is the only one who calls me that. "Thanks buddy."

"I hope it makes your head feel better."

My heart could practically burst. "I bet it will."

Climbing from the couch, I make my way over to the island. "Let me try this."

I take a huge bite, letting the sweetness melt on my tongue. "Best cookie I've ever had."

"You hear that mama?" Trace bounces on his toes. "I make the best cookies."

Laiken chuckles. "Well then where's mine?"

"Patience, mama," he says sternly.

A warm heat washes over me from behind. Cooper leans over my shoulder to snatch a cookie. "I think I need to be the judge."

He shoves the whole cookie in his mouth, crumbs dropping onto his boots as Trace giggles uncontrollably.

Laughing, I reach for a napkin, waiting until he chews before I wipe the pink icing from the corner of his mouth.

He smirks, leaning down to drop a kiss on the tender spot behind my ear. "Thanks, baby."

I freeze, as a gasp filters behind me and Ruthie's eyes widen.

Uh oh.

Cooper seems oblivious to what he just did, causing the entire room to bring their sole focus to us. You could hear a cow *moo* ten miles away with how quiet the cabin is. I'm about to blurt out something stupid. Anything to explain away the silly comment when my phone rings. I thank the Lord for the interruption and collect my phone from the counter.

"Hello."

"Dakota, it's Jefferson."

"Hey. Did you find who ran us off the road?" I ask.

Immediately, Cooper slides his hand around my waist, dropping down on a bar stool. He tugs me between his spread thighs, eyes watching mine.

"No, unfortunately not. But that's not why I'm calling. I did some checking. It looks like the letter regarding your father's pending release was mailed to the address *126 Cherry Drive* three weeks ago."

My heart drops.

"That's my old address," I say, my entire body turning rigid. "What are you saying?"

"I'm saying your father was released from the Cove County Correctional facility two weeks ago."

The phone slips from my hands, my legs nearly buckling. Cooper recovers it, bringing the phone to his ear.

"What happened?" He growls.

He pauses, before he nods. "We'll call you tomorrow."

When he hangs up, he never moves his eyes from mine. My worst nightmare was coming true. He was free. And he was coming for me.

Chapter Forty-Five

Cooper

"Is this necessary?" Ryder asks for the third time.

"If you ask me that again, I'll punch you in the fucking face," I threaten before climbing down from the ladder.

I had already installed a camera at the front entrance. One at the barn. Two in my cabin, and now we're putting a couple at the main office where Maddox and Ivy do the majority of their work. We had a minimal security system. We never had issues with anyone breaking in. But all that changed when I heard Billy Sterling was walking free. *Was he here?* His exact where abouts where still unknown, and Jefferson assured me they were working on it. It had already been four days, and I was having a really hard time letting Kota and Ari out of my sight.

"I get it man." Ryder picks up a screw gun. "I'd do the same thing." He pauses. "Well, I mean you know what I'd really do to solve this problem."

I'm aware my brother has zero fucks to give. Which is why if I gave the word, he would end Billy Sterling, no questions asked. But having him in prison, or anyone else in my family for that matter isn't a valid option.

"I appreciate the offer." I swipe at my brow with my forearm. "But I don't think murder is the way to go."

He shrugs. "Just a thought. In case you need a plan B."

I stare at my brother. I know there's more to what he's been through in his life to make him so aloof. So *cold.* But he doesn't share. And I've never forced him to. That's how we work.

"You want to come to Ari's birthday party next weekend?" I ask, moving the ladder to the other end of the building.

"A teenage girl's birthday party. Sounds right up my alley," he mumbles, following behind me.

"Good. It starts at four. We're doing cake and ice cream then taking her to the festival."

"I never said I was going," he says before he pulls out another camera from the back of the ATV.

"Dakota thinks it would be good for her. Get her mind off the accident and the custody stuff. I don't think she was ever able to just be a normal kid, you know?"

"Like Dakota?" He asks, handing me the camera.

"Yeah." I swallow. "Can't let that happen to her. Not after I wasn't able to keep Kota safe."

"You did keep her safe." He fires back. "Always have."

We both work in silence after that, neither of us knowing how to articulate how we feel. It feels heavy, and once we finally get the last camera attached, we call it a day. Dakota wasn't going to like what I had planned for her, but if she gave me any lip, I'd just kiss her until she agreed.

End of story.

"A deal is a deal."

Ari narrows her eyes, before she crosses her arms.

"Am I right?" I ask as I hold the reins to Buster.

"You told her how you feel?" She questions.

And then some.

"Yes." I motion my hand. "Now you have to ride a horse."

An angry snort, followed by a frustrated neigh echoes from the arena behind us. The sound of Dakota's cursing has me holding in a chuckle. She's working with one of the new colts today. He's turning out to be a problem horse. But if anyone can break him, it's her.

"One time around the pen," Ari tosses out.

"Nope. You have to get a feel. At least five laps."

"Five!" She shrills.

"Do you trust me?"

She opens her mouth, then closes it. "You don't play fair, Papa C."

"Come on. Let's surprise Kota." I move Buster near the fence. "This will make her day."

"Fine. But only because I count on you for my meals."

With a chuckle, I guide her to the fence. "Just climb up here and we'll get you on. He's pretty tall so we can work on your form later. I just want you to be comfortable in a saddle."

Her blue converse sneakers carry her up the pipe fence, before she faces Buster. "If something happens to me, I want Trace to have my sketchpads." She blows out a breath. "And Ivy to have my bath bombs."

I snicker and hold out my hand. "I'll make sure to get your last will and testament filed with the county before dinner."

Her small hand takes mine, her eyes darting from Buster's face, back to the saddle.

"Just swing that leg over, and hold on to the saddle horn," I instruct.

After a brief hesitation, she flings her leg out, then lunges forward to land in the saddle with an *umph.*

"Great. Now sit up straight and try to get in the center." I walk to the front of Buster and pat his neck.

"Like this?" She asks.

"Perfect." I turn. "We'll go slow, and I'll lead you around. He can't go anywhere in this round pen, and honestly, he'd rather sleep than be out here."

I begin to walk, keeping my eyes on Ari as we make the first round. She seems to visibly relax by the third, and by the fourth, I swear she cracks a smile.

"What is going on out here?" Dakota comes to the fence, a smile on her face and dirt smudged on her cheek.

"Just paying a debt," Ari says casually.

"A debt?" She questions.

I laugh, stopping to give Kota a quick peck on the lips when we pass. She blushes, her eyes flickering up to Ari.

"You don't have to get all bashful, Dakota. I know he's your Hus."

"My Hus?" She laughs.

"Yeah. Like for real though. Not a fake Hus," Ari says as we make the last round.

"Ok then." Dakota smiles. "Yeah. He's my husband. For real."

When our eyes meet, I see the pride she holds as she looks up at Ari. "You're a natural."

Ari snorts. "I wouldn't go that far. But it's kind of nice."

"See?" I pause, moving Buster closer to the fence. "Five rounds. Not too bad."

Ari climbs off the saddle, then down the fence until she drops on the ground next to Kota. "He's your problem now. I've got homework to do," she says before she jogs toward the barn.

"Think she'll come around?" Dakota asks.

I lean my elbows on the pipe railing. "She'll come around. When she's ready."

Dakota smirks. "Must run in the family."

I slide my arm through the rail, snaking it around her waist. "Don't worry. I can be patient with my girls."

My girls.

She smiles. "I like the sound of that." Then her plush lips meet mine.

Chapter Forty-Six

Dakota

I can sense Cooper's glare on the side of my face as we pull into the Briar Bar Ranch.

"I don't know why you're so mad at me. You're the one who insisted on tagging along."

"For your safety," he mutters.

"And I'm sure Ryder was thrilled you backed out on moving the herd."

"We came to an understanding," he says as he shifts in his seat.

"Well, you better be nice." I narrow my eyes as we pull up to the arena. "He pays a lot of money for me to train this horse."

Cooper mumbles under his breath as I put the truck in park. Truthfully, I was glad I had a client today. It got my mind off my father, and all the ways this whole situation could go south. Jefferson had multiple officers working on tracking him down. In the meantime, I just had to stay alert. Watch my surroundings. I needed to work, and the last thing I wanted while on horseback was worrying about Cooper and Dean Vickerson getting along.

When I climb out of the truck, Cooper has already managed to make it to my side. He crowds me against the warm metal, his cologne making me wish we were curled up in bed instead of heading into this arena.

His fingers grip my chin, before he tilts my head back. "You realize I'm not trying to be a dick, right? I just want you safe. If anything happens to you..."

"Hey." I reach up and bring his forehead to mine. "I'm right here. Nothing is going to happen to me."

He blows out a slow breath before he leans in, his lips pressing to mine. "I know."

He kisses me slow, before I open, letting his tongue slide inside of my mouth. His leg wedges between my thighs, the pressure sending a warm sensation straight through my core. We hadn't gotten another chance to repeat what happened in the hotel room since we've been back, but I've been aching to feel him again.

A whimper escapes my throat, my hips rolling as he slides his hand up to gently grip my throat. "Kota."

"Mhm," I hum.

"We need to stop."

I nip at his lip, knowing he's right.

"I'm about three seconds away from fucking you against this truck and over my dead body will Vickerson get to watch."

When he says his name, I remember why I'm here. *I'm a professional.* I press my palms against Cooper's chest, before I clear my throat.

"You're right." I smooth down my shirt. "Let's get to work."

I slowly lope the beautiful paint mare around the arena, cooling her off. She worked hard today, and she's making great progress. I glance over to the fence, but Cooper is nowhere in sight. He must have taken a phone call.

A slow clap sounds from the end of the arena, so I whip around to see Dean walking toward me. I nudge her into a trot, meeting him just at the entrance of the gate.

"Excellent," he says, dropping his hands on his hips.

"I'd say she's almost ready to start working with cattle." I pat her neck.

Dean smiles beneath his hat, his brown beard moving with the expression. "It's all because of you."

"I won't take all the credit." I run my fingers through her mane. "This girl was easy to teach."

Dean has always been a little flirty, but I really believe it's just his personality. I've seen him in action plenty of times, but I've never mixed business with pleasure.

Swinging my leg over the saddle, I dismount just as I hear a familiar growl.

"Care to explain why you're ogling my wife's ass, Vickerson?"

Chapter Forty-Seven

Dakota

Dean's eyes widen as Cooper stares daggers at him.

"I was doing no such thing," he denies, then he frowns. "So, it's true? You married him?"

"Yes, she married me." Cooper smirks.

"Dean," I say, trying to deescalate the situation. "She did great. I'm thinking another month and she'll be ready." I hand him the reins. "I have another appointment, but I will be back next week."

"Thanks, Dakota," he says, cutting his eyes at Cooper who looks like someone stole his candy bar.

I give Dean a wave, then shoot Cooper a pointed look. "Let's go."

My boots cut through the dirt, then through the barn that leads to my truck. I can feel Cooper hot on my heels, his steps frustrated.

"What the hell was that?" I hiss as soon as we get into the cab.

"What?" He scoffs, slipping his hat off. "He can't look at you like that."

"Oh, so are you just going to act a fool with anyone who looks my way?" I ask as I pull out onto the road.

"Damn right. It's disrespectful."

A smile tugs at the corner of my lip, because it's rare I see Cooper ruffled. He's always sunshine and smiles. Never jealousy. It's kind of.... *hot.*

Spotting a turnoff that leads to an empty field and an old gas pad, I take a right, veering off onto the desolate road.

"What are you doing?" He sits up taller.

I whip the truck beside a cluster a trees, parking before I unclip my belt and climb over the console.

When I straddle his lap, naturally, he reaches down and slides the seat back.

I wrap my arms around his neck. "Cooper." I lean in and kiss him, my tongue lapping against his.

"Kota," he murmurs against me.

"I've had a rough couple of days. I'm stressed. I'm tired. I'm nervous. And right now, I don't want to feel any of those things." I rock my hips against the bulge hardening in his jeans sitting just below my center. "I want to feel you inside me," I whisper.

As soon as the words float between us, he captures my mouth with a groan. His hands tangle in my hair as my fingers go to my jeans. It takes practice and flexibility to peel the jeans from my body and shuck my boots, but somehow, I do it with grace. I reach for his button, and he lifts his hips, shoving his pants down his thighs.

His fist grips his length, his eyes wild as he tugs me in for a searing kiss. I feel his tip line up at my entrance, the plush skin stretching me as I slowly ease down.

A moan leaves my mouth, while his head tilts back to land on the head rest.

"Kota," he grits out. "Ride me"

I begin to move, my hands resting on his shoulders, my nails scratching against the material of his shirt. His hips rise to meet mine, every thrust driving deeper. Every movement bringing us closer. Tingles run from the tips of my toes to the tops of my ears, warmth and love spreading through my chest as his eyes latch onto mine. So blue. So much love. So...*mine.*

"I love you," he says, his hands gripping my hips. "Fuck, I love you."

"I love you too," I gasp, my muscles clenching.

One hand slides up under my shirt, before I reach down and tug it over my head. My breasts are covered by a black bra, the material thin enough to showcase my pointed nipples.

His finger catches on the cup, tugging it down to expose my bare skin.

With a groan, he leans forward, capturing my nipple in his mouth. He sucks hard, the zing from the contact shooting down to my clit.

"Touch yourself," he rasps against me. "I want to feel you fall apart."

My hand snakes down between us, my fingers strumming as I ride him in my front seat in broad daylight.

His nostrils flare, his eyes bright as his palm reaches up to lightly grip my throat.

One more thrust and I'm tumbling. Falling and spinning. I cry out his name, before I feel his release, then collapse on his chest. With heavy breaths, I close my eyes, wondering why we waited so long for this. So long when it could have been *this* good.

"Not to ruin this intimate moment," Cooper whispers. "But do you have any idea how many times I dreamed of fucking you in this truck?"

I snort, then slap at his chest as I sit up. "How many?"

"An embarrassing amount," he admits with a laugh.

Pressing a kiss to his lips, I slowly slide off of him, then grab my jeans. "Just for the record. You're the first."

He stills. "First what?"

"First for my truck." I say, keeping my eyes trained on maneuvering my foot in my pants.

"Good." I can hear the smile in his voice before he adds. "I better be the last."

Chapter Forty-Eight

Cooper

My hand slides around Dakota's waist before I drop a kiss on her exposed shoulder. "Morning."

"Morning." She smiles at me through the mirror, right before she pulls out a tube of makeup.

"So, Christine is coming to the party?" I ask, before grabbing my boots.

"Yes." She drops the tube, then curses.

"There's nothing to be nervous about," I tell her.

It's been a quiet week in terms of reckless drivers and threatening notes. Ari has had a good week at school, and we even arranged for Heather to meet us at the fall carnival to surprise her. She has no idea we're throwing her a party at Ivy and Maddox's house. It was too risky to do it here, and when Christine called to see about coming for a final home inspection, we thought it would be a perfect time for her to meet the family. *Ari's family.*

"I know." She braces her hands on the counter. "I just want this birthday party to be the best."

After slipping on my boots, I push to my feet.

"Hey." I wrap my arms around her shoulders and lean my chin on her head. "You're doing an incredible job with her. I know you're trying not to push her. To let her open up when she's ready. She loves school. I even find her sneaking out to the barn to see the horses. She's thriving." I press a kiss to her hair. "Thank you."

She spins to face me. "For what?"

"For letting me keep my word."

She raises up on her bare toes, pressing a kiss to my lips. "You've always been my hero, Coop."

"And you've always been my queen of chaos." Her head tilts back in laughter. "Let's go. Maddox and I are on balloon duty."

Three hours later, balloons, streamer, and a buffet style pizza palooza is taking over Ivy and Maddox's living room. The cake is displayed at a small table in the corner with a huge blowup *13* in gold floating up behind it. Me, Maddox, Ivy, and Laiken are huddled in the kitchen, hiding behind the island. The rest of the crew is hunkered down in the living room. It's been all hands on deck today, and I was even surprised Clyde was willing to help. He's taken it upon himself to teach Ari the art of rolling your own tobacco. Which frankly I'm not sure if it's a good history lesson, or a disaster waiting to happen. He means well, but we had to give Ari the big *just say no* speech to smooth it over.

My phone dings, signaling that Dakota and Ari are in route.

"They're coming," I whisper. "Get ready."

Dakota knocks twice on the back door, acting as if she's completely clueless to what's waiting on the other side. When she swings the door open, she slides to the side while we all spring up shouting, "surprise!!!"

Dakota grins, her hands coming up to cover her mouth as Ari gapes at the room. Her eyes bounce around, landing on every face before she stops on the two tiered cake and balloons. Her face morphs from shock, to blank in a matter of seconds, followed by a trembling lip.

Oh no.

One second, she's standing with wide eyes, then the next, she's bolting out the door.

Chapter Forty-Nine

Dakota

Crap.

I give a sympathetic look to the group, before I go after Ari. My heart breaks at the thought of making her cry. Was it too much? Did she hate birthdays? The sounds of her sniffles lead me to the barn, where she's leaned against the stall, petting Rebel. Cooper had mentioned he saw her sneaking down here, but I hadn't seen it with my own eyes. And right now, she reminds me more of myself than she ever has. Sneaking down here to see these horses was my safe haven.

"Hey," I say gently. "You ok?"

Her eyes are trained on Rebel, a few tears rolling down her pink cheeks. "I'm sorry."

"What do you have to be sorry for?" I lean against the wall to the tack room and cross my arms. "If I overstepped, I'm sorry."

"You didn't." She sniffs.

"Talk to me," I urge softly.

"I just..." she sighs, then turns to peer at me over her shoulder. "I've never had a birthday party before."

Oh, my heart.

"Or a cake. Or balloons." She pauses. "A family."

"Ari." I take a step and wrap my arms around her. "It's ok."

"I'm sorry I ran. I don't like anyone to see me cry," she admits.

"Reminds me of someone else I know." Cooper saunters over, his big arms coming out to wrap around us both. "What has my girls crying in the middle of the barn?"

"Just a little overwhelmed," I whisper.

He shoots me a wink over her head. "I'm a little wounded you didn't like my balloons. I practically gave up a lung to make that arch."

Arizona chuckles and untangles from my grasp. "I love the balloons, Papa C."

"Good." He squeezes her shoulder. "You alright? We don't have to go back in if you don't want to."

"I do." She nods.

"She just needed a minute," I offer.

Ari's blue eyes shine with moisture as she swipes at her face. "Ok. I'm ready."

"And only because it's your birthday." I give a pointed look. "There's a pizza with an ungodly amount of pineapple on it calling your name."

Her smile brightens. "Sick."

"There's not a single piece left," Ruthie says as she gathers up the empty pizza boxes.

"I'm pretty sure Ryder ate an entire box by himself," Ivy says before elbowing him in the ribs.

"I was starving. Try being up all night with a sick heifer," he grumbles.

We spent the last two hours eating, laughing, and watching Arizona open her gifts. It was so heartwarming to see her genuine smile and gratitude. She hugged every neck, even Christine when she got here. We were able to introduce Christine to the whole family, and even with the shadow of my father lurking, I think she sees how well Ari fits with us.

"Ok. We have one more gift," I announce, smiling at Cooper.

He shoots me a wink, then opens the front door. "Follow me."

Ari follows, as I slowly lag behind, walking the path back to our house. How we managed to pull off a complete room remodel in the small amount of time we had available was a miracle. All thanks to Emmett and Ryder.

When Cooper leads her inside, she glances over at me in confusion. "Are we going to the guest room?"

Cooper presses a palm against the bedroom door. "Nope. We're going to *your* room."

Ari freezes when she steps into the doorway. A brand new dresser sits on the back wall, which is a beautiful pale blue. The new bedspread is a quilt material with lightly painted feathers. Whips of colors and strokes of a paintbrush decorate the material to give it an artistic vibe. A new drawing desk sits in the corner, along with a lamp and a new sketchbook with a set of pencils. And the kicker, which I haven't even seen until now, is the frames. My throat swells when I see the three framed drawings hanging on the wall.

"Coop," I whisper.

His fingers intertwine with mine as Ari and I stare at her drawings. One is of Rebel. A beautifully shaded drawing of his profile. The other is of Buster as he drinks from a trough. Then the last one, the one that has tears forming in my eyes is of me and Arizona. We're walking on what appears to be two different roads, but one arm is outstretched, our fingers linking over the space.

"Ari, these are beautiful." I blink.

"Those are my favorites." Ari looks back to Cooper. "How did you know?"

"I see you, Ari," he says simply.

"Thank you." She gives a watery smile. "It's perfect."

Before I can reply, she spins around, her arms flinging up as she dives at us. Laughter echoes between us as we hug our girl.

"This is the best birthday ever," she whispers.

I grin. "And guess what?"

She pulls her head back. "What?"

"It's not over yet."

Chapter Fifty

Cooper

Heather and Arizona laugh hysterically as the teacups spin another circle. The carnival is in full swing, reminding me of so many times I brought Dakota here. How I punched that asshole Rhodes when he hurt her feelings and when I almost kissed her on the Ferris wheel when we were seventeen.

A soft hand curls around my arm, and I peer down to see my wife smile up at me. "You ready to take me on a ride, cowboy?"

My hand slides down to snake around her narrow waist. "I got something you can ride," I murmur into her ear.

She chuckles. "This is a family friendly event, Cooper."

"The parking lot isn't," I mutter.

"Dakota!" Arizona waves a hand. "Can we ride the avalanche?"

"Sure." Arizona and Heather dart out of the gate and onto the next ride.

Slipping Dakota's hand in mine, we walk through the crowd, passing Trace and Laiken as she videos him on the mechanical bull.

"You know. I never thought I'd get to be at this carnival holding your hand," she says, her voice full of emotion. "And here we are. Married."

I tug her to me. "The Ferris wheel?"

She glances around. "Ivy!"

Ivy turns to face us with Maddox at her side.

"Can you keep an eye on the girls while we ride the Ferris wheel?"

"Of course!" She waves.

I'm already yanking Dakota to the line, giddy as fuck that I'm about to make out with my wife like a fifteen year old teenager with a crush.

The elderly man opens the gate, allowing us to filter out to the carts. We take our seat and drop the latch.

"I always love when we get to the top," she admits. "The view is something else."

The clank of the machines and the happy screams of the children below sound as we begin to ascend. My arm rests on the cart behind Kota's back as we watch the distant crowd.

"I love you, Cooper," she says quietly, looking out over the carnival.

"I love you, too." My fingers gently caress her shoulder.

She turns to face me, her expression serious. "I know you didn't sign up for this. That you married me to help me. And yes, I know you love me, but this is big. If I get custody...." She clears her throat. "I don't want to force you into something you're not ready for. Being a parent. To someone that's not even your child is a huge responsibility."

"Hey." I grip her chin lightly. "I know exactly what I signed up for."

"Do you?" She asks. "You're ok with teenage hormones? My cleaning sprees. Mean girls. Tears. School dances. Training bras, because we know that's coming next."

I can't help the laugh that expels from my chest. "You think I wasn't there to experience every single one of those things with you?" I give her chin a slight shake. "I'm practically a professional at this point. I love the chaos, Birdie. And I love you. Which means, I love all the parts of you. And that little girl is a part of you. So yes, I know what I signed up for." Her eyes glisten as I lean in closer. "And make no mistake, baby. When I offered to marry you, I wasn't just doing a good deed. Being a good guy. I saw the chance to make you mine. To show you just how much love you deserve. So, if a life with you and Ari is what you are offering me? Then yes. Sign me the fuck up."

Her laugh echoes around us, her head dropping to rest on my shoulder. "Cooper Mayson you do have a way with words."

I press a kiss to her forehead. "Now, if you'll stop second guessing everything, I want to kiss my wife on a Ferris wheel."

Chapter Fifty-One

Dakota

"Did you see me?" Trace asks, his face lit up like the Fourth of July. "Rode that bull a full eight seconds."

"You did?" I ruffle his hair. "I bet you scored more points than Parker," I tease.

"No one gets more points than Parker," he says as he adjusts the huge belt buckle on his jeans.

"Is there a reason we are bringing up *him*?" Laiken asks.

I lift a brow, waiting for her to continue. Which she doesn't. Laiken can be as closed up as they come. She thinks I don't see that something obviously happened with her and Parker at some point in time. But she hasn't disclosed a single detail. She just rolls he eyes or changes the subject when his name comes up. *Interesting.*

"He's riding in the championship next weekend." Trace fist pumps. "Gonna kick some ass."

"Trace!" Laiken hisses.

"Damn right he is," Maddox chimes in.

"You are not helping," Laiken scolds.

"Come on buddy. One more game and it's closing time." Maddox grabs Trace by the waist, hoisting him over his shoulder.

"Those two." Ivy laughs. "I think my ovaries explode every time I see them together."

I laugh, letting the image of what a baby would look like for me and Coop. Would he want more kids? We already have a teenager.

Definitely didn't see that coming.

"I need to use the bathroom really quick. Let Coop know I'll be right back," I tell Ivy.

Moving through the crowd, I give Fern a wave as she waits in line for a corn dog. Of course, she gives me a scowl before turning away. I almost laugh, but I bump into a tall figure.

"Oh sorry!" I apologize, before stepping around him and up to the portable trailers. Whoever invented a portable bathroom that has AC, I would like to personally shake their hand. There is nothing worse than peeling blue jeans off your sweaty ass when you need to urinate.

The line moves quick. I can't help but smile as I watch a little girl about four with pigtails attempt to wash her hands while wildly reenacting her pony ride. It's precious, and for the first time, I actually feel like that was something that was in reach.

When I exit the trailer, the cool autumn air hits my face. The days may still be warm, but the evenings are when it feels the best. Texas rarely gets a fall. It's either scorching hot or freezing cold. The in between is sporadic, and rare, so I always take advantage. Tonight would be a great night to ride out to the ridge.

When I take a step, my phone buzzes in my pocket. I expect a text from Cooper, but the *unknown* name is what stops me cold.

I gulp, pausing to swipe the screen.

My heart stops. My world crashing when I open the screen to see a picture of Arizona. On the teacup ride. My hand trembles as another comes in. One of her and Cooper laughing by the popcorn stand. And the last is a picture of me standing at the trailer, looking down at my phone. *Shit.*

Panic hits as I swivel my head.

Another buzz.

Unknown: Maybe they should pay for your sins.

Bile rises in my throat as I whirl around. That picture was taken from behind me. I scan the crowd, the faces blurring. Walking to the side of the trailer, I peer behind it, checking to see if I can see anyone fleeing. Seeing if my shitty father would be a coward or not. *Coward it is.*

My fingers fly over the screen, sending a text to Cooper.

Me: Get Ari out of here. Now.

As soon as the text is sent, the hair on the back of my neck stands up. Tension rolls down my spine, my senses spiking as I hear the rustle of grass behind me. Before I have a chance to turn, an arm wraps around my neck from behind, then something sharp presses into my ribcage.

"You scream and the girl gets it."

A gasp shoots from my mouth, not because of what he said, but because of who said it. It wasn't my father's voice in my ear.

It was Dean's.

Chapter Fifty-Two

Cooper

I switch the stick of cotton candy over to my other hand while I fish my phone out from my pocket. When I swipe the screen, I frown at the text from Dakota.

Kota: Get Ari out of here. Now.

Sudden dread sweeps over me as I immediately survey the area. Arizona is standing a few feet from me, her and Heather comparing the goldfish they won at the last game.

"Girls," I say, my tone causing Arizona to furrow her brows.

Motioning them to me, I quickly tap Dakota's name. It rings four times before going to voicemail.

Shit.

"Hey. They're closing up. We better get out there before we're stuck trying to leave," Maddox calls as he and Ivy walk up.

"What's wrong?" Ivy must see the worry on my face.

"I'm not sure." I clear my throat. "Maddox. I need you to take Heather home. Then take Ari back to your house at the ranch."

He holds my gaze for only a few seconds before he jumps into action. "Alright girls. Load up."

Ivy watches me closely. "Where's Dakota?"

I lower my voice. "I need to find her."

"Hey." Laiken and Trace join us, her hand holding tightly to his.

I meet Maddox's eyes, the unsaid words passing between us.

"Laik, I need you to meet us at the ranch," he says calmly.

"Why?" She asks. "It's Trace's bedtime and he..."

"Laiken." Maddox's tone changes, before he swaps another silent look with her. "Please go to the ranch."

"Come on, Ari." Ivy plasters on a smile, trying to keep things calm for the girls.

Arizona stands next to me, her face scrunching. "Where's my sister?"

I reach out to squeeze her shoulder. "Bathroom. We'll be right behind you."

Arizona may be only thirteen, but she's got more street smarts than any adult I know.

"Something's wrong," she states.

"I'm not sure." I shake my head. "But I need you to go with Ivy and Maddox. Please."

For a second I think she's going to argue, but she nods before following my sister out of the entrance.

My chest tightens as I glance around. The carnival is clearing out, and I'm searching for that familiar long, dark hair. My boots move across the field, aiming toward the bathrooms.

I toss the cotton candy in a nearby trash can before I reach the portable trailer. A woman is sweeping the staircase. "Ma'am," I call to gain her attention. "Can you check if my wife is in there, please?"

"Sure, hon." She yanks open the door, poking her head in. "Anyone in here?"

When there's apparently no answer she comes back out. "Sorry, it's empty."

"Thanks."

My gaze darts around.

Where are you, Kota?

She wouldn't just leave. I know her. And she must have felt Ari was in danger. But why?

Fire lights in my veins. The thought of Billy possibly showing up. Of scaring her.

I pull my phone out again, scrolling to her location. The blue dot shows her to be here. Still at the carnival. I exit out, then dial her number again. The faint sound of a phone ringing echoes in the dark. I swivel around, trying to locate the source.

Another ring.

Moving to the side of the trailer, I glance around the back, and that's when I see it. Lighting up in the dirt.

Her phone.

"Fuck," I hiss as I stride toward it.

Swiping it off the ground, I go to her calls. Nothing out of the ordinary. No unknown numbers. Then I open her text messages.

And that's when I realize.

He's been watching. He was here. And my worst fucking fear may have just become a reality.

He took her. He took my wife.

Chapter Fifty-Three

Dakota

My head pounds as I attempt to peel open my eyes. The room before me is a blur, but the smell is unmistakable. Crazy, I haven't stepped foot in this place in years, and I can tell by one inhale where I'm at.

I'm in hell.

The stench of stale cigarettes brings back a flash of memories. Ones I'd buried beneath my broken heart. Ones I'd promised I wouldn't let erase the woman I'd become. But sitting here, the memories whip around me like an unexpected hurricane. Fast and relentless.

When my eyes adjust to the dim room, the first thing I spot is the broken down couch. The same one my father used to pass out on after he drank too much whiskey. I thought it was odd no one ever moved into this trailer after he went to prison. But according to the red spray paint that's displayed across the front door reading *tainted,* it's no surprise.

"There she is." The voice to my left has me shifting my eyes.

I lift my legs to move, but my hands are tied behind my back.

Perfect.

"Dean." I lean back against the warped paneling. "Didn't peg you for the bondage type."

"Then I guess you misjudged me," he says smugly, standing from the chair at the metal kitchen table.

"Care to share what this is all about?" I ask calmly.

Dean was a few years older than me, so I didn't know him well outside of the horse business or a random social setting. His family's ranch was well known. Aside from the rumors that his father had made some financial decisions that were questionable, they appeared to be getting along just fine. I mean, they hired me. I never went there with Dean. *And I'm beginning to see why.* Honestly, I didn't go there with many men contrary to what my friends think. Just because there's some flirting and a little two stepping, it often stopped there. Or in front of my trailer when I was dropped off. I was ok with them thinking I was living a single cowgirl's dream. I didn't want them to know how much it hurt to know I'd never be the woman that Cooper Mayson took home. *Or so I thought.*

"Cooper Mayson? Really?" He scoffs.

So that's what this is about? A grown man throwing a hissy because he didn't get picked for the team?

"How mature." I roll my eyes. "Ego take a hit, Dean?"

He stalks forward, his hands clenching at his sides. "I've never had a woman reject me. Never." He paces across the room. "Married. Single. Widowed." He glares at me. "They always want me."

Wow. Arrogant much?

"But not you," he sneers. "You think you're better than me? That because you can ride a fucking horse and have a Mayson eating out of the palm of your hand my bed is not good enough?"

He's practically yelling, his eyes wide with anger. I've never seen him act this way. He's always the cool cowboy. Throwing winks and tossing lines.

"Is this really about me?" I tilt my head. "Sounds to me like it's not that I don't want you. It's that I chose a *Mayson* over you."

"They think that ranch is so fucking special." He kicks the coffee table, snapping a leg in half. "What? They have a few bulls that are worth a shit and now have some big name." He crouches down next to me. "That entire ranch should have burned down with that house."

I twist my wrists, trying to loosen the rope as he stares daggers at me. "He may get that ranch, Dakota. But he doesn't get you too."

He's even more deranged than I thought.

"What are you doing?" I ask. "What's the point of all this? You know I won't go willingly."

He reaches out to trail a finger along my jaw before I jerk away from his slimy touch. "I'm glad you asked."

My nostrils flare as I narrow my eyes. "Don't touch me."

"Oh, I plan on doing more than touching you." He grins, the gleam in his eyes unsettling. "First, we're getting revenge, then, you're coming with me."

I swallow thickly, my brows furrowing. "We?"

The rattle of the trailer door makes my blood run cold, and when it opens to reveal the monster that I'd thought I'd slain, my world stills.

The door slams as the tall figure fills the space. He's older now. Grey streaking his greasy hair. His eyes are hollow, matching the gaping hole in his chest where a heart never formed.

My monster is back.

His smile is sickening before he announces. "Daddy's home."

Chapter Fifty-Four

Cooper

"What's going on?" Ryder climbs down out of his truck, a blank expression as usual.

I called him the second I found her phone, along with Jefferson who's standing next to me and my father in the empty parking lot of the carnival.

"Dakota is missing," I grit the words out with an ache I can't shake. "She texted me to get Ari out of here, then when I went to find her, all I found was her phone in the dirt. She wouldn't just leave. Especially without this."

"Ok." Jefferson, yanks on his pants. "Is there anywhere she would go?"

"I'm telling you she didn't leave on her own." I feel my dad lay a calming hand on my shoulder.

"Did we locate Billy?" He asks.

Jefferson shakes his head. "Not yet. It's like when he left Cove County, he disappeared."

"You try Joseph? He used to work with Billy," Ryder inserts. "Those low lives are two peas in a pod."

"Someone sent her these." I hand the phone to Jefferson. "Can you trace it?"

He glances at the picture and curses. "Shit."

Ryder mutters under his breath and my dad starts to pace.

"This is a clear threat." I motion. "We need to find her. I know it's Billy. He's the only one with a reason to hurt her."

"Let me get this back to Duncan. Otis isn't in the office so I can push it. I know Billy worked for Rocky, I don't want him to try to intervene."

Otis Bernard is Rocky Bernard's brother. But just because he was the *sheriff* didn't mean he was on the right side of the badge.

"How fast?" I urge.

"I'll head to the station now, you can follow me," Jefferson says, before he pulls out his radio.

I glance at my father. "I'm not sitting around."

"I know, but we need to let them do their...."

Ping.

Dakota's phone pings, and Jefferson's face pales when he sees the screen.

"What?" I bark.

"We have a problem." He turns the screen to me.

I'm not prepared for the sight in front of me. I'm not prepared to see the love of my life, wrists bound, mouth gagged, lying on dingy green carpet. The text that reads below is what has me nearly buckling to the dirt.

> Unknown: Two hours. Ridge Race Track. $500,000 cash. Bring the money or she pays. With blood. No cops.

"How the fuck does he expect us to come up with that kind of cash?" I scoff, before yanking open the door to my truck. "Like I would even give it to him if I had it."

"Where are you going, Cooper?" My dad asks, his tone serious.

"To the trailer." I slide into my seat. "I'd know that nasty carpet anywhere."

"Shit," Ryder mutters. "I'll go with you."

"Boys," my dad scolds.

We lock eyes. He knows I'm going after my wife regardless of what he tells me.

"You two go." He motions. "I'll go with Jefferson. Work on the money."

With his quick nod, we spin out, slinging dirt behind my truck as we head to the highway.

"What's your plan?" Ryder asks.

"Kill that fucker and get my wife back." I turn right, racing down main St.

A few heads turn as we zip past, but my eyes are focused on the sign about half a mile up the road. *Mayson Ridge Mobile Home Park.*

"Don't do anything stupid, Coop. She may not even be there."

My hands grip the wheel, my skin hot as we sail through the entrance to the park, gunning it to the fifth trailer on the right.

When I slide to a stop, we both jump out, our boots pounding on the overgrown lawn as we rush the trailer door. My hand finds the knob first, and I practically rip it off the hinges when I storm through.

"Kota!" I shout.

The living room is empty, along with the kitchen.

"Kota!" I call again as Ryder heads to the back.

Nothing. She's gone.

My palm rubs against my chest; the ache back as I survey the room.

My eyes catch on something along the carpet. Crouching down, I squint, letting my fingers dust over the tint on the fibers.

Is that......

Blood.

"Cooper. You need to see this," Ryder says, his voice hoarse.

I'm still staring at my hand. At the blood coating my fingertips.

"Coop."

I glance up before pushing to my feet.

"What is it?"

He turns, heading to the hallway, then stops at the bathroom door.

I mentally prepare myself, my lungs working double as I join him near the frame.

A sharp breath hits me. "Fuck."

"Yeah." Ryder pulls out his phone. "I'm calling Jefferson."

Dean Vickerson's body lies in the tub. A gunshot wound to his head.

Falling back against the wall, I try to process. To figure out what piece Dean is in the puzzle. But only one thing matters right now.

He hurt my wife. *Again.* And this time, he's getting more than a prison sentence to pay for his sins.

Chapter Fifty-Five

Dakota

My scream echoes through the trailer when a bullet hits Dean in the middle of the forehead.

Billy barely gives him a glance before he tucks the gun back in his jeans and looks around like he's in some nostalgic state.

"Idiot," he mutters.

"What the hell, Billy?" I shriek. "What's wrong with you?"

He waves a hand dismissively. "I didn't need him anymore."

He takes him by the ankles, dragging him down the hall and to the bathroom.

"Anymore?" I question, my stomach churning at the fact that I've been around him all of thirty seconds and he's already committed first degree murder.

Billy strides back down the hallway, then to the old fridge, checking inside with a grunt before he turns his soulless eyes back to me. "You think I left without eyes on you? That I'd just let the little bitch that put me inside get away with it?"

"You had him watching me?"

"Yeah. Had him toy with you a little too." He laughs. "I'll admit it. I didn't think he had it in him to run you off the road."

My stomach sinks. It was Dean?

"I couldn't risk the law seeing me. He owed me."

I shake my head. "He was practically a kid when you went to jail."

"A kid with connections. Needed someone to keep up my part in the trade while I was inside."

I shift, still working the rope on my hands.

"Trade?"

He runs a hand over his hair. "Drugs, Dakota. How else do you think I paid rent on this piece of shit."

I wince when he picks up an old beer can and tosses it against the wall. "And you had to fuck it all up. With your lies."

"You just admitted you were dealing," I point out. "How is that my fault?"

"You testified!" He shouts.

I try to move quick when he lunges for me, his hand wrapping around my throat. "You told the cops that was my bag," he grits out.

I gasp, my throat burning as he squeezes tighter. "Did eight years for your bullshit. You're no better than your old man. Lying for your own gain." He chuckles before he lets go of my throat. "Too busy letting that Mayson boy spread your legs to be grateful for everything I gave you."

My cough is painful before I glare up at him. "What you gave me?" I cough again. "Fuck you, Billy."

I should have known it was coming. He backhands me hard across the cheek, causing me to fall to the floor. My face meets the old carpet, before he's in my ear.

"I may have been dealing, but that wasn't my fucking bag." He presses a hand on my face, forcing me against the floor. "Dean wasn't supposed to be doing a drop off that night. Looks like he couldn't follow simple directions either."

He lets go of me, and my cheek throbs.

"All you ever had to do was keep your mouth shut." He growls. "Live up to the Sterling name. Never thought my own daughter would be a snitch."

"I never thought my own father would be a worthless piece of trash but here we are."

When he grips my hair, and tugs me up, I let out a mangled scream. From pain and anger. From fear and frustration.

"Don't bite me," he warns before he pulls a piece of cloth from his back pocket.

He spins it a few times before shoving it in my mouth, tying the ends behind my head.

With no emotion, he shoves me to the floor then he pulls out a phone, snapping a quick picture before he types on the screen. A wicked smile slips into place after he shoves it in his pocket.

"Turns out you might be good for one more thing before I toss you like I should have when your mother left," he mutters while yanking me up to my feet.

He drags me behind him, crossing the living room to the front door. "For some reason the Mayson's seemed to have taken a liking to you. I have a feeling he'd pay a pretty penny to get his wife back."

My stomach burns, bile rising in my throat at the thought of Cooper. At the trouble I'm bringing right to the Mayson's door. *To Ari.*

I shake my head *no,* trying to talk through the gag.

"I beg to differ."

My arms ache as he opens the passenger side door to Dean's truck, ushering me inside with a force that makes my shoulders burn. The angle of my arms is making it hard for me to maneuver my body, but I still haven't stopped working the rope. I can feel it loosening each time I twist my wrists.

He cranks the engine and smirks. "Let's make a trip back to our old stomping grounds."

Billy places the gun on the console.

"Don't make me use this." His threat is followed by the shift of the truck.

Gritting my teeth, I peer out the window, seeing if anyone is outside. Of course, the one night I need a witness there isn't a soul in sight.

We pull out onto the main road, and the only thing saving me right now is the darkness. It gives me the opportunity to finish untying my hands. My mind spins, multiple plans forming as I mentally sift through which is plain stupid or worth it. Most of them would be plain stupid, but I never claimed to be smart. I do, however, claim to be fearless. I claim to be a woman who never backs down and will fight like hell to leave behind the life that tried to destroy me. I think about Arizona. About the life we can give her. About the world she deserves. One where she can draw sunsets and use fruit loops as vengeance. Where she can expect a warm meal and her own room. I think about Cooper. *My Cooper.* I finally know what it feels like to lay in his arms. To be the one he showers with love and grace.

Billy Sterling isn't going to be the one who takes that away from me. Not now. Not ever.

Which is why instead of sitting quietly like a good little victim, I bite the inside of my cheek, then use all of my strength to snap the remaining twines of the rope.

He doesn't notice, he's too busy mumbling to himself, while I casually relax my arms.

Damn those hurt.

I take a small breather, watching as we leave the Mayson Ridge city limits. A stretch of darkness surrounds us, and I know my time is running short. The farther away from town, the longer I'll have to get back. There's only going to be one way to stop him.

Saying a quick prayer, and channeling my inner badass, I make my move.

My hands dart out quick, snatching the gun from the console. He reacts a little too late, swerving as I point the barrel at him. The sudden jerk of the truck has me crashing against the door, my hand colliding with the headrest which catapults the gun to the back seat.

His voice is a roar as he swerves away from the ditch, overcorrecting as we travel across the opposite lane.

It all happens so fast. One second, we're on asphalt, and then the next, we're tumbling.

And everything goes black.

Chapter Fifty-Six

Cooper

"Where the hell are they?" I seethe, my boots pacing across the parking lot of the track.

When we didn't find her at the trailer, we came directly here. Knowing that asshole would do anything for a buck, I was certain he wouldn't flake. Billy Sterling was as crooked as they came. So the fact he wasn't sitting in this parking lot, waiting on his demanded $500,000 was alarming.

Ryder picks up his phone.

"What are you doing?"

"Calling Jefferson," he grits out. "I'm done with this bullshit."

Ryder had notified him about Dean, and officers had the place swarmed by the time we left. He had agreed to have him and three other squad cars nearby while we waited for Billy to show up. We didn't have much of a plan, or his money, but I was getting my girl back regardless. We'd use force and manipulation if necessary.

"We need a trace. Now. He's still not here," he barks into the phone.

He's silent for a moment before he hangs up. "He said it should be within ten. Techs are working on it. He could be using a burner."

Something in my gut tells me this isn't right. That he wouldn't just demand we show up then bail. But this *is* Billy. What if he just wanted us to be distracted while he got out of town. *While he took her with him.*

A flash of light flickers across the lot as Jefferson barrels out of a squad car.

"We have a problem," he says, his strides long. "Got a trace. Pinged at the trailer first. Last location was on the highway right outside of town, then it disappears."

"Just like that?" Ryder asks.

"Just like that. Either he turned it off or threw it out the window. Something."

"It doesn't make sense." I pull off my hat and run my fingers through my hair. "We need to physically check the last location," I call out, already on the move to my truck.

"We'll follow you," Ryder calls before he gets behind the wheel.

When we all file out of the parking lot, I still can't erase that gnawing feeling that we're missing something. And it may be too late.

"This is it?"

Jefferson nods. "Yeah. It ends here."

We're parked on the highway that's leading out of Mayson Ridge.

"I can't see shit," Ryder scoffs. "There's no way we're going to find a phone in all this overgrown grass."

The fact it disappeared doesn't sit right. He was only about ten miles from the track. Why would he not show?

Walking along the road, I shine my phone light on the asphalt looking for anything. A sign.

Where are you, Birdie?

Then I see it. Skid marks. Ruts in the grass. I shine my light farther out, across the ditch that separates the road from the drop off.

Shit.

The guard rail that acts as the barrier to the river below has a chunk missing.

The tension along my spine nearly snaps me in two when I see the trajectory.

"Ryder!" My voice breaks as I charge toward the guard rail.

The black night is thick, but as I shine my phone over the edge of the drop off, a small shiny light reflects back at me.

A taillight.

Chapter Fifty-Seven

Dakota

A gasp leaves my throat, my eyes popping open as a cold chill skates over my body.

Blinking my eyes, I immediately hear the rushing of water surrounding me. My vision is spotty, my eyes straining to adjust to the dark. The only light is the one shining from the cracked radio screen.

My head feels heavy, accompanied by a sharp pain in my right leg. I lift my hands, peeling the material away that is still lodged in my mouth. When I suck in a sharp breath, the scraping of metal sounds as the truck shifts. I brace my hands, realizing why my head feels like it's about to explode.

We're hanging upside down.

The truck shifts again, the drop causing a scream to rip from my throat when water begins to filter inside of the cab. Craning my neck, I see Billy hunched over, a gash on his head, and blood trickling from his mouth. I don't have time to figure out if he's conscious or not. The fact the vehicle is submerging into what appears to be the river has my survival mode kicking in. Taking a breath, I quickly survey the cab. The windshield is still intact but has a small diagonal crack. My head is cramped near the top of the cab, so I slide my hands down the door, feeling for the handle in the dark. I know I need to get out. And fast. I pull the lever, my shoulder shoving against the door. But it doesn't budge. It's wedged against something solid on the outside.

I try again, slamming my shoulder into the door. *Nothing.*

As the water rises, so does my pulse. *Think, Dakota.*

I scan the windows, my gaze going back to the windshield. If I can just get it to shatter, I can swim out.

Maneuvering my body, I lift my aching leg, the pain sharp as I kick with all of my strength.

Nothing.

I kick again.

And again. And again.

Nothing.

I scream out, the cold water rising over my torso.

"Cooper!!!!!" I scream as the heel of my boot strikes the glass.

Tears prick my eyes as the water reaches my shoulders.

"I need you," I choke out, knowing he won't come.

He doesn't know where I am.

The weight of the water sits on my chest, forcing a gasp from my mouth as my hands fumble for the door lever again.

"No. No," I mumble.

He doesn't get to win. Billy Sterling doesn't get to win like this.

Another cry leaves my throat, a panic rising as I try to kick at my window.

That's when I realize, he's won.

One more breath fills my lungs before the water engulfs my entire body.

Letting the realization settle in my bones, I let my mind go back. Back to a time when a little boy saw me. *Really saw me.*

His golden hair.

His blue eyes.

The peace he brought while I was in the middle of the storm.

Suddenly, his face appears. So real it's like he's here. Like he found me.

Thud

My eyes close.

The faint sound of my name being called through the rush of water.

Thud.

My chest aches.

Thud.

I'd give anything for one more moment.

Anything.

I drift off with a singular promise.

I'll always love you, Cooper Mayson.

Chapter Fifty-Eight

Cooper

My thumb casually strokes against Dakota's hand. The one that has an IV taped against her smooth skin.

She lays peacefully in a hospital bed, still looking like the most beautiful thing I've ever seen.

"You need to get that hand looked at," my mother says quietly, placing a kiss on the top of my head. "It looks gnarly."

When we spotted the truck down in the ravine, it took us nearly fifteen minutes to get to it. Then it felt like it took a lifetime until I was hauling my unconscious wife out of the submerged vehicle. My fist beat that windshield until it finally shattered and I was able to get her out.

By then, the ambulance and fire crew had been called. Brady was on shift, and I couldn't respect him more for how he took charge, barking orders left and right before she was transported directly to the hospital. That was nearly ten hours ago, and she still hasn't woken up.

The doctor said sometimes the body needs time after a traumatic event. Like nearly drowning after a horrific car accident.

"My hand is fine," I dismiss.

"Hey, Papa C." I turn at Arizona's voice.

"Ari." I open my arm, welcoming her for a hug.

I know she's been worried sick.

She comes immediately, squeezing me tight.

"Is she going to leave me too?" She whispers.

The question sends a spear through my heart. "No," I answer, pulling back to look at her. "She's a fighter. Most stubborn woman I know."

She nods, her eyes full of worry.

"Son," my father calls from the doorway, his expression filled with empathy.

"Would you like to sit with her a minute?" I ask Ari.

She nods her head, taking my seat as I stand. My whole body hurts as I stretch my back.

"You can touch her, sweetheart," my mom tells Ari with a hand to her back.

I catch eyes with my father, following him into the hallway.

"Everyone is down in the waiting room. Even Ryder."

I rub my eyes, trying to keep myself in check. She has no idea the amount of people that love her.

"You doing ok?" He asks.

I scrub a hand across my face. "I just need her to wake up. Hear her voice."

I stare at the linoleum, my mind racing. *Guilt* flowing through my veins. Guilt of how this is all *my* fault.

"I can tell what you're thinking." He squeezes my shoulder. "Don't go there."

I lean back, sagging against the wall. "He wanted revenge dad." I have to pause to gather my wits. "Revenge for something she didn't even do."

He steps closer, his face lowering to my ear. "You did what you had to do to protect her."

I remember his exact words from eight years ago. They made sense then. The catalyst behind what we crafted. We *had* to, to protect her. And getting Billy out of Mayson Ridge and away from Dakota was the only way.

I protected her.

But at what cost?

He steps back and his eyes hold mine.

I feel myself breaking. The weight too much.

His voice lowers. "You had no idea she'd be in the truck that night."

Even though his words are true, it still stings. I didn't know she'd be with him the night I snuck that backpack full of drugs into Billy's backseat. I had no idea she'd be in the truck when I made the phone call about a reckless driver. And I had no idea that she would see an opportunity, just like I did, and take it.

"We do whatever it takes for the people we love. I'd give you that money all over again if it meant it put that mean bastard away and gave her the peace that she deserved. And if she would have known it was you, that knowledge would have hurt her more than helped her."

My throat clogs, the emotion stomping my chest. If she dies.... If she loses her life because of my choices.

"He's gone, Coop. Billy Sterling will never get to her again." He puts both palms on my shoulders. "Some things are meant to be left in the past."

I hold his gaze, letting what he's saying sink in. All that matters now is that Billy Sterling died in that car crash. And my wife was finally free.

Chapter Fifty-Nine

Dakota

Six weeks later

"How do I look?" I ask, running my hands down the lace gown that had me crying the first time I saw it.

"Total baddie," Arizona says with a smile.

"Are you sure?"

"Totes. The Hus is going to flip." She wags her brows.

She opens her arms. "How about me?"

"Gorgeous as usual."

"Staaapp," she mocks embarrassment, flipping her hair.

"Come here." I open my arms to her, and she steps in immediately.

We've made leaps and bounds when it comes to mine and Ari's relationship. She's even opened up about Bea's death and has joined in on the days the advocacy center comes out to the ranch.

"Love you." I squeeze her tight.

"Love you too, D."

I've officially been gifted a nickname, and it makes me smile every time.

Arizona Larue Sterling was officially deemed part of our family three weeks ago, and the paperwork has been filed to complete the transition to make her a Mayson. As for now, we're fluttering around Ruthie and Emmett's new farmhouse preparing for my wedding.

My real wedding.

The last six weeks have been a blur. Between me almost drowning, spending three days in the hospital, being granted full custody of Ari, and planning a legit wedding, I've been nothing but smiles and exhaustion.

After getting a lengthy lecture from Cooper about my actions the night of the accident, he immediately dropped to one knee right there in the hospital room, asking me to marry him in front of the entire nursing staff and our family. The nurses were confused, but everyone else had already caught on weeks ago.

A knock sounds at the door, whispers filtering through as Ivy and Laiken amble in. They both freeze, hands flying to their mouths.

"Oh my God," Ivy fans her face. "I'm going to cry."

"Me too," Laiken sniffs. "You look stunning."

"Why are you crying, mama? I thought Aunt Ivy only cries since she has a human in her tummy."

"Trace!" Laiken shrieks.

My eyes widen. "What!!!!"

"Shhhhh." Ivy flails her hands.

"Maddox." Laiken calls down the hallway. "Can you take him please?" She cracks the door, shoving Trace out. "And please explain to him how we keep a secret."

She shuts the door and I'm still gaping at my best friend. *Well, sister-in-law.*

"You're pregnant?" I ask.

"Yes." She looks remorseful.

"And you didn't tell me!" I gasp.

"It's your wedding day!" She shrills. "We found out yesterday, and I didn't want to ruin your day."

"Ruin my day?" I roll my eyes. "Ivy Mayson. First of all. I'm already married, and I would have been completely content on keeping the courthouse ceremony the only wedding we had. But we both know your brother is dramatic and wanted the whole shebang."

She laughs, swiping tears from under her eyes.

"And second. This little rugrat is my niece or nephew. I'm over the moon for you."

Ivy is full on crying now as I cross the room to her.

"Trace is a little sneak and must have overheard us this morning." Laiken laughs as she joins us in a group hug.

"I'm so happy for you," I tell her.

"Maybe you'll be next." Laiken teases.

I glance back at Ari who's putting on lip gloss. "Please, mine's already potty trained and knows how to do dishes. I'm golden."

Another knock sounds at the door and we disperse, all wiping our eyes.

Ruthie pokes her head in. "It's time."

Stepping onto the front porch of the farmhouse, I glance out at the yard that showcases rows of white chairs that hold our closest family and friends. A beautiful arch of wildflowers sits at the end of the aisle, along with Cooper, Maddox, and Ryder.

"I'm ready, Kota," Trace says, a turquoise pillow resting on his tiny palms that hold our rings.

"Ok. It's your turn," Laiken urges him forward. "Go stand by Uncle Mads."

He proudly stomps down the stairs, then down the aisle. Arizona follows, dropping white petals along the way. Next is Ivy and Laiken, their gorgeous blue long sleeve dresses perfect for this December weather.

"You sure you want to marry him? I got a horse saddled out back if you want to run." Emmett smiles, stepping up next to me in his starched jeans and button up shirt.

A little yellow flower is pinned on the pocket.

I tilt my head back on a laugh. "I think I'm finally done running."

He holds out his elbow. "Then let's get you down that aisle."

Chapter Sixty

Cooper

I have to cover my mouth with my hand, clearing my throat when Dakota steps in my line of sight. My father escorts her toward me, a bright smile painted on her pretty face. I feel Maddox clap a hand on my shoulder as I blow out a breath.

The soft music flows from a speaker somewhere in the yard, the instrumental melody filling the air. When Dakota reaches me, my dad places a kiss on her cheek, then places her hand in mine. He nods his head at me, and I move my gaze to hers. Those blue eyes I fell in love with all those years ago shine back at me.

I love you she mouths, her eyes sparkling.

I mouth the words back as Ernie steps up next to us.

"I'm getting Deja Vu," he says before a chuckle vibrates from beneath his sweater vest.

The crowd laughs, and I wink at Dakota.

Ernie flips open his bible, then begins the ceremony. I don't really pay attention. All I can do is stare at the woman I have the privilege of calling my wife. A woman that is now a *mom*. A woman who looks like the dark shadow that's always followed her is long gone, and she's free to soak in the light.

"If I remember correctly. You said your vows last time." Ernie gives Dakota a pointed look. "Do you have yours this time?"

"I don't think we need to repeat those, Ernie." I smile. "I think we meant them the first time." I take both of her hands in mine. "I know I did. Every single vow."

"Okay then. The rings?"

We both take the rings from Ivy and Maddox, doing the exchange the same as before. Only this time, I have one more ring in my pocket.

I peer around Dakota. "Arizona could you come up here please?"

She points at her chest. "Me?"

"Yeah, you." I chuckle.

She slips around Laiken, then walks up to stand next to Dakota.

Kota grips her hand in hers, her eyes full of tears.

I crouch down. "Today I'm not just making a promise to Kota. I'm making one to you." I pull out the small silver ring. "You may not have been with us since birth, but you came into our lives in the most unexpected and perfect way. Like you were always meant to find us. We love you. And I want to give you this to symbolize that I vow to be everything a father should be. I vow to love you. To teach you. And to run off any hairy legged boy with a shot gun that asks you on a date."

Laughter erupts, and Ari smiles, but tears still stain her cheeks. She reaches out to take the ring, sliding it on her finger.

"Thank you," she says before launching herself in my arms. "I love y'all too."

When she pulls away, she wraps her arms around Dakota, before she goes directly to Ivy's side, I push back up to my feet while Dakota smiles at me, her head shaking in awe.

"Well, if there is nothing else. By the power vested in me by the state of Texas, you are once again, pronounced husband and wife. You may kiss your bride."

This time my girl is ready. I take off my hat, wrap an arm around her waist, and kiss the woman of my dreams.

Epilogue

Dakota

Three weeks later

"Where's Ari?" I ask, stepping into Cooper's office.

"Her and Ryder rode out to the ridge," he says, glancing up from his desk.

"I'm speechless."

He leans back in his chair. "I think it's hilarious."

I walk inside, then perch on the edge of his desk. "I think she's going to break him out of his shell."

"I think he just finally realized she won't take no for an answer." He moves his legs, wheeling over to position himself in front of me.

"I don't know. Ryder may not be as grumpy as he lets on."

"Oh, believe me. He's grumpy as fuck." Cooper laughs before his hands land on my thighs. "You know." He runs his palms up higher, ghosting his fingertips very close to the seam on my jeans. "Everyone is out right now. We have this barn all to ourselves."

"Oh really?" I lean back to rest my hands on his desk. "What do you suggest we do about it?"

He grins, pushing up from the chair to cradle my face. "I think I should strip you down." He presses a kiss to my lips. "Bend you over this desk."

I nip at his lip, my hand sliding over the denim of his pants. He's hard as steel.

It's been a little tricky to navigate alone time while living with a teenager. She's not naïve and we'd like to not scar her for life if possible.

His lips slant over mine, his tongue stroking against me as I unbutton his pants and pull down his zipper.

A hum sounds in the back of his throat as I reach inside to pull him out.

My palm wraps around his shaft just as someone shouts. "Anyone here?!"

"Shit," Cooper curses, stepping back before he's tucking himself inside of his pants.

I roll my eyes when Parker appears in the doorway.

He pauses, his eyes bouncing between us. "Did I interrupt?"

"Nope," I say, as Cooper mutters, "yes."

Parker grunts something under his breath while I slide off the desk. "What brings you to Mayson Ridge?"

He opens his arm for a hug, giving me a quick squeeze. "Sorry I couldn't be at the wedding. Surgery was brutal."

Parker won the championship at the finals, but before he could leave the arena, a collision had him sustaining a concussion, four broken ribs, a ripped rotator cuff, and a jaw fracture.

"It's ok. Maybe you'll be at our next one." I pat his back. "We've already had two."

His chuckle his gruff, just like the rest of him.

Cooper motions to the duffle bag in his hand. "You staying?"

Parker gives him a look. One I'm not exactly privy to. It seems like some inside conversation between the two cousins.

"Ruthie said the loft was open." He shrugs.

Cooper studies him a moment. "Just you?"

Parker nods. "Just me."

"Alright." Cooper shoves his phone in his pocket, then strides to me. "Let me get him settled then we can finish our conversation."

I can't help but smile when he leans down to brush a kiss across my lips. "Promise?"

He slaps a hand across my ass. "Promise. Now get out of here."

I leave the office, heading to the cabin that's now cheerfully decorated with Christmas lights. Ari even convinced Cooper to build a life size Santa sleigh, reindeer included.

My foot is planted on the first step when I see a car coming down the drive. Laiken skids to a stop, then dives out of her SUV.

"What's wrong?" I frown.

Laiken never gets mad. *Like ever.*

"Laiken?" Parker stands at the edge of the barn, his brows furrowed.

Laiken glares at him before facing me.

Her hand lifts, a finger pointed directly at the infamous bull rider. "*That,* is what's wrong."

The End.

Thank You

Thank you for reading ***Every Single Vow***, book two of the ***Every Single Series***.

Wonder what happened between the infamous bull rider and the single mom?

Parker and Laiken's story is coming soon!

A second chance, single mom, cowboy romance!

For other books or information on release dates and all things S .J. Chaynie, visit **www.authorsjchaynie.com** to sign up for my newsletter or follow me on social media.

My Tribe

First off, I had so much fun with this book! Cooper's sunshine personality was refreshing after writing some grumpy heroes (but I still love them). Dakota's story was heartbreaking at times, and I found myself with tears in my eyes as I wrote her flashbacks. And Ari. Ari was inspired by SJM. My very own preteen who loves to draw, uses words I don't understand, and has more wit in her pinky finger then I've had in my whole life. She's been asking "when will I be in a book?" It's your time to shine, sister! Mayson Ridge is such a fun place, reminding me so much of my hometown. Thank you to everyone who played a role in making this book possible. My family for dealing with my character background lectures and my late-night editing phases. Thank you to AB. The queen of keeping me on track and listening to my wild ideas and plot crisis'. Thank you to my MIL who takes time to help me edit, to my Street Team who gets my book out into the world with your words and support. Thank you to my ARC readers, and anyone who took the time to sit down and dive into this world. I appreciate each one of you and I am forever grateful!

About the author

S.J. Chaynie is a small-town Texas girl who has found a love for writing. She enjoys writing romance, with a sprinkle of suspense, and a little humor. If she is not busy writing her newest ideas, she is spending time with her husband and two beautiful daughters. She believes a good book and a lot of laughs is the best medicine. She brings suspense, love, angst, and sometimes the occasional heartbreak to her stories. Always a HEA, but every character and story she holds close to her heart and hopes they touch yours as well.

Printed in Dunstable, United Kingdom

74828659R00168